Samuel French Acting Edition

Woman of the Year

Book by
Peter Stone

I0591881

Music by
John Kander

Lyrics by
Fred Ebb

SAMUELFRENCH.COM   SAMUELFRENCH.CO.UK

ISBN 978-0-573-68117-2

www.SamuelFrench.com
www.SamuelFrench.co.uk

FOR PRODUCTION ENQUIRIES

UNITED STATES AND CANADA
Info@SamuelFrench.com
1-866-598-8449

UNITED KINGDOM AND EUROPE
Plays@SamuelFrench.co.uk
020-7255-4302

Each title is subject to availability from Samuel French, depending
upon country of performance. Please be aware that *WOMAN OF
THE YEAR* may not be licensed by Samuel French in your territory.
Professional and amateur producers should contact the nearest Samuel
French office or licensing partner to verify availability.

For all enquiries regarding motion picture, television, and other media rights, please contact Samuel French.

MUSIC USE NOTE

Licensees are solely responsible for obtaining formal written permission from copyright owners to use copyrighted music in the performance of this play and are strongly cautioned to do so. If no such permission is obtained by the licensee, then the licensee must use only original music that the licensee owns and controls. Licensees are solely responsible and liable for all music clearances and shall indemnify the copyright owners of the play(s) and their licensing agent, Samuel French, against any costs, expenses, losses and liabilities arising from the use of music by licensees. Please contact the appropriate music licensing authority in your territory for the rights to any incidental music.

IMPORTANT BILLING AND CREDIT REQUIREMENTS

If you have obtained performance rights to this title, please refer to your licensing agreement for important billing and credit requirements.

CAST OF CHARACTERS

TESS HARDING
GERALD — Tess' secretary
HELGA — Tess' housekeeper
CHIP SALISBURY — A network anchorman
SAM CRAIG
PHIL ⎫
ELLIS ⎪
ABBOT ⎬ Cartoonists, Sam's friends
PINKY ⎭
MAURY — A saloonkeeper
TONY — A doorman
PRESCOTT — An F.B.I. agent
ALEXI PETRIKOV — A Russian ballet dancer
LARRY — Tess' first husband
JAN — Larry's wife
and A CHAIRWOMAN, other COMMITTEEWOMEN, TV TECH-
NICIANS, PATRONS of Maury's tavern, and OTHERS.

MUSICAL NUMBERS

ACT ONE

"WOMAN OF THE YEAR"
"THE POKER GAME"
"SEE YOU IN THE FUNNY PAPERS"
"WHEN YOU'RE RIGHT, YOU'RE RIGHT"
"SHUT UP, GERALD"
"SO WHAT ELSE IS NEW?"
"THE POKER GAME" (Reprise)
"ONE OF THE BOYS"
"TABLE TALK"
"THE TWO OF US"
"IT ISN'T WORKING"
"I TOLD YOU SO"
"WOMAN OF THE YEAR" (Reprise)

ACT TWO

"I WROTE THE BOOK"
"HAPPY IN THE MORNING"
"SOMETIMES A DAY GOES BY"
"THE GRASS IS ALWAYS GREENER"
"OPEN THE WINDOW, SAM"
"TABLE TALK" (Reprise)

Woman of the Year

ACT ONE

SCENE 1

[MUSIC NO. 1 — OVERTURE]

Backstage at a hotel ballroom. There is a curtain, up, separating us from the ballroom itself.

AT RISE: [MUSIC NO. 2 — OPENING]

An awards ceremony is in progress. Seen through the curtain, a dais on which sit SEVERAL WOMEN in formal attire and, at the center, her back to us, standing at the lectern, the CHAIRPERSON, her voice amplified.

On this side of the curtain: a very large, blown-up photograph of TESS HARDING.

CHAIRPERSON. — This year's winner, with her intelligence and wit, her skill and talent, her charm and glamour, has not only achieved a phenomenal success as a broadcast journalist, a field heretofore dominated by men, (*fanfare*) but she has also, through her blissfully happy marriage to the well-known cartoonist, Sam Craig, (*fanfare*) proven beyond all doubt that today's woman can be successful both in her career *and* her marriage —

(*Now, a STAGEHAND enters and picks up the large photo, carrying it off — and thereby revealing the real TESS HARDING who's been standing behind it.*)

TESS. (*She sings.*)

"WOMAN OF THE YEAR"

SAM CRAIG
WHEREVER YOU ARE
LISTEN, YOU SON OF A BITCH
LISTEN TO THAT!

CHAIRPERSON.
— THIS GRACIOUS, WELL-KNOWN PUBLIC FIGURE
WE'VE ADMIRED FOR SO LONG—

SAM CRAIG
WHEREVER YOU ARE
YOU ARROGANT, ILL-TEMPERED, BRUTISH,
INSENSITIVE
CHAUVINIST SON OF A BITCH
LISTEN TO THAT!

CHAIRPERSON.
— HER VAST ACHIEVEMENTS IN THE MANY FIELDS
OF HER ENDEAVOR—

TESS.
IT'S MY NIGHT, SAMMY
ALL MINE, SAMMY
AND YOU CAN'T GIVE IT
YOUR WELL-KNOWN WHAMMY!

CHAIRPERSON. (*speaks*) — This award tonight must come as something of an anti-climax to a person who's already won a Pulitzer Prize, two Peabody Awards and two Emmies—

TESS. Three Emmies—

THE LADIES ARE
  SINGING MY PRAISES
SOON, THEY'LL BE
  RAISING THE ROOF
I'M NOT GOING TO
  LISTEN TO YOU, SAM
WHY SHOULD I
  LISTEN TO YOU, SAM?
WITH THIS

INCONTROVERTIBLE	GIRLS.
PROOF!	CHRIP A CHIRP A CHIRP
(*spoken*)	CHIRP
Speak up, girls!	CHIRP A CHIRP A CHIRP
	CHIRP
Don't be shy!	CHIRP A CHIRP A CHIRP
Speak up!	CHRIP A CHIRP A CHIRP
Do you hear that,	CHIRP A CHIRP A CHIRP

Sam!?   CHIRP

(*singing*)
YOU DON'T NEED TO BE
  HAPPY
OR SERENITY ITSELF   CHRIP A CHIRP CHIRP
YOU DON'T NEED ANY
  PHOTOS
OF NIAGARA ON THE
  SHELF   CHIRP A CHIRP CHIRP
YOU DON'T NEED ANY
  HUSBAND
GRINNING FROM EAR
  TO EAR
TO BE THE WOMAN
  OF THE YEAR   CHIRP A CHIRP A CHIRP
                             CHIRP CHIRP
                             CHIRP A CHIRP A CHIRP
                               CHIRP

YOU DON'T NEED TO BE   OH--------------------------------
  STARKERS
IN A PLAYBOY CENTER-
  FOLD   CHIRP A CHIRP CHIRP
YOU DON'T NEED ANY   OH--------------------------------
  DOCUMENT
TO PROVE YOU'RE NOT
  THAT OLD   CHIRP A CHIRP CHIRP
AND YOU DON'T NEED A
  HUSBAND
 LEADING A PUBLIC
  CHEER
 TO BE THE WOMAN OF
  THE YEAR

 WHAT YOU NEED IS
  BRAINS
 WHAT YOU NEED IS
  PUSH
 WHAT YOU NEED IS
  ENERGY
 TO GET YOU OFF YOUR
  TUSH   CHIRP CHIRP
 BUT YOU DON'T NEED

MEN,
WHEN YOU COME TO BAT
NO YOU DO NOT NEED
  A MAN,
I'M THE PROOF OF
  THAT!   CHIRP A CHIRP A CHIRP
                                 CHIRP CHIRP
                                 CHIRP A CHIRP A CHIRP
                                   CHIRP

YOU DON'T NEED A
  VILLA
OR A NEW GLASS TOWER
  SUITE   CHIRP A CHIRP CHIRP
YOU DON'T NEED A
  CHINCHILLA
AND I HAPPILY REPEAT: CHIRP A CHIRP CHIRP
YOU DO NOT NEED A
  HUSBAND
MANAGING YOUR
  CAREER
TO BE THE WOMAN
  OF THE YEAR

WHAT YOU NEED IS
  GUTS
WHAT YOU NEED IS
  HEART   CHIRP CHIRP
AND YOU NEED THAT
  MOVE AND SHAKE
TO MAKE YOUR MOTOR
  START
BUT YOU DON'T NEED
  MEN   MEN
TELL THEM ALL
  "NO SALE!"   NO SALE
EVEN IF YOUR FEET GET
  COLD
ON THE OLD
  PERCALE   CHIRP A CHIRP A CHIRP
                                 CHIRP CHIRP
                                 CHIRP A CHIRP A CHIRP
                                   CHIRP

YOU DON'T NEED ANY BLOODLINES	OH-------------------------------
GOING BACK TO GOD-KNOWS-WHEN	
YOU DON'T NEED A TIARA	OH-------------------------------
AND I'LL SAY IT ONCE AGAIN:	
YOU DON'T NEED ANY HUSBAND	OH-------------------------------
I DID NOT NEED A HUSBAND	
I WANT TO MAKE THAT VERY CLEAR	

SO, SAM CRAIG, WHER-
  EVER YOU ARE
THOUGH YOU THINK
  I'M A SHAM
TAKE YOUR POW! AND
  SHAZAM!
AND GO SHOVE IT AND
  SCRAM
'CUZ GODDAMMIT, I AM
THE WOMAN—

  CHAIRPERSON. Ladies and Gentlemen, Miss Tess Harding—

TESS.	GIRLS.
—OF THE YEAR!	CHIRP CHIRP
	CHIRP A CHIRP A CHIRP
	CHIRP CHIRP
	CHIRP A CHIRP A CHIRP
	CHIRP A CHIRP A CHIRP
	CHIRP!!!!

Listen to that!!

[MUSIC NO. 3A—WOMAN PLAYOFF]

(*After song: TESS now steps through the curtain and acknowledges their applause.*)

TESS' VOICE. (*recorded*) Thank you, thank you. I accept this honor with pride and gratitude. You know, it's only been a few years since this award was given for a bright smile and a clean kitchen. Well, we've come a long way baby—

(*During the above speech, as the figure of TESS, through the curtain, continues to acknowledge her award, the actual TESS suddenly returns backstage—the figure behind the curtain is a DOUBLE—and expresses to us her innermost thoughts.*)

TESS. Well, he spoiled it. He really spoiled it. I was looking forward to this but now I'm not enjoying it at all. What did I need him for? I was doing just great on my own, why'd I have to screw it up? If I hadn't shot my mouth off that morning on the show we never would have met. When was that, eight months ago? My God it seems like eight *years!* (*She turns and walks off as the lights fade.*)

TESS' VOICE. (*continued; now faded*) [—I know I certainly have. And I owe it all to television, a medium that opened its doors to me, allowed me to express my views, made me new friends all over the world, and was even responsible for the way I met my husband—]

TV ANNOUNCER'S VOICE. (*off, in the dark*)—Coming up after a word from your local stations—the "Early Bird" show from New York, with anchorpersons Tess Harding and Chip Salisbury—

(*The curtain opens to reveal:*)

SCENE 2

A TV studio, set up for a network early morning show; there's an anchor desk with two chairs, several monitors and a large clock.

AT RISE: *NUMEROUS PRODUCTION PERSONNEL are scurrying about, preparing for the show.*

FLOOR MANAGER. Fifty seconds to air—fifty seconds!—
DIRECTOR'S VOICE. (*amplified, off*) Where the hell's Tess?! Somebody check her dressing room!—

(*Now CHIP SALISBURY, a handsome anchorman with sprayed hair, enters.*)

CHIP. You mean she's not here yet? I don't believe it! (*calling off*) *I need a spritz!* (*A HAIRDRESSER will arrive and start spraying and arranging his hair.*)

FLOOR MANAGER. Forty-five seconds—!

CHIP. Forty-five seconds! My God, she's always pulling something like this!

DIRECTOR'S VOICE. (*off*) It's okay, she's here!

CHIP. Where? I don't see her.

(*GERALD, TESS' secretary, an extremely serious, dedicated man, enters.*)

GERALD. She's fixing her hair.

CHIP. Sure. That's just like a dame. Where the heck has she been?

GERALD. In a limousine, driving in from the airport.

CHIP. You'd think she could at least get here on time.

GERALD. She *was* on time. The plane was late.

FLOOR MANAGER. Forty seconds—!

(*HELGA, TESS' housekeeper, a solidly built Germanic woman, enters, carrying a garment on a hanger.*)

HELGA. Gerald! Where is Miss Harding? One minute I was beside her and the next I was beside myself!

(*TESS now enters—she's dressed in a one-piece jumpsuit.*)

TESS. It's all right, Helga, here I am.

HELGA. Gott sei dank! I thought you were verschwinden!

TESS. Please, Helga, in a civilized language. Gerald, you'd better cancel my lunch with Teddy—I can't get down to Washington before three.

GERALD. Already done. I rescheduled for Friday.

(*During this, HELGA will take the garment—it's a dickie-like blouse that fits over her jumpsuit and ties in the rear—it will give her a more feminine look when she sits to face the cameras.*)

FLOOR MANAGER. Thirty seconds—!

DIRECTOR'S VOICE. (*off*) Tess, are you doing an editorial? We don't have any copy—

TESS. (*calling*) Don't worry, I wrote it in the back of the car.

FLOOR MANAGER. Twenty seconds to air . . .

GERALD. Miss Harding, don't you want to wait until you can smooth it out a bit — ?

TESS. Why? What's wrong with it?

GERALD. You might upset a few people —

TESS. That's what editorials are for, Gerald.

GERALD. If you'd only hear me out —

TESS. I hear you, I hear you. Everything will be just fine.

FLOOR MANAGER. Fifteen seconds, clear everybody.

CHIP. Holy cow, Tess — you're cutting it a little close, aren't you? Only . . .

FLOOR MANAGER. . . . Ten seconds.

TESS. Sorry, Chip — I was down in the Bahamas interviewing Prince Andrew.

CHIP. Prince Andrew? No kidding. That guy's quite an operator. Was Koo there?

TESS. (*a beat*) Koo who?

FLOOR MANAGER. — two — one — (*He points at TESS as she just manages to slide into her chair and smiles at the camera.*)

TESS. Good morning and welcome to Early Bird. I'm Tess Harding, along with Chip Salisbury. It's seven o'clock here in New York and we've got a fascinating two hours lined up for you today — Chip, why don't you tell everybody about it?

CHIP. Hm? Oh, sure. Love to, Tess — let's see, uh — (*picking up a page*) From Washington, an interview with my old buddy, Speaker of the House Tip O'Neill — I guess that's *your* old buddy, Tess, I've never met the man — (*passes the page to her*) — and then, to round out this first half hour, the ever-delightful Pia Zadora. But first, to our Early Bird newsroom for the latest news and Scott Chichester. Scott — ? (*The red light goes out and everyone prepares for the next set-up.*) Look at my hair! (*shouting off*) I need a spritz! (*The HAIRDRESSER will reappear and start to work on him.*)

TESS. (*observing him*) You know, Chip, the only thing that makes me doubt television is the fact that you're on it.

[MUSIC NO. 3B — T.V. PLAYOFF]

FLOOR MANAGER. Fifteen seconds to air . . . fifteen seconds . . .

(*SAM's studio now moves on — a cartoonist's workroom, filled with the equipment of the trade — a drawing board, cups filled with pencils and pens, bottles of ink of all colors, rolls of paper, sheets of cardboard, etc. Four men — PHIL, ELLIS, ABBOTT and PINKY — cartoonists, are seated around SAM's worktable, playing poker. In the fifth chair sits a large, overstuffed animal — KATZ, SAM's cartoon character, holding five cards in one hand. From the look of things they've been playing all night.*)

ABBOTT. Come on, Katz, it's your bet. We're waiting on you, as usual. Katz!

PHIL. Sam, it's up to Katz!

SAM'S VOICE. (*off*) Katz raises five bucks!

PHIL. (*staring hard at KATZ*) You're bluffing, Katz. I can tell from your face you're bluffing. I call.

PINKY. Okay, I'm in. What've you got?

PHIL. (*laying down his cards*) Three jacks.

PINKY. (*throws his down*) Beats me.

PHIL. What've you got, Katz? (*SAM enters, carrying a small TV set. As he passes behind KATZ, he peeks at his hand.*)

SAM. Read 'em and weep.

PHIL. A flush?! (*He grabs the hand away from KATZ, then shakes his head.*)

SAM. (*Laughing, he continues past, setting the TV set DS., its back to us.*) Aren't you guys getting tired of feeding the kitty?

PHIL. I know I am. When I get skunked by a stuffed cat it's time to quit.

PINKY. Oh, sure, you're still ahead a few bucks so you want to cut short the game!

ABBOTT. Short?! It's seven o'clock in the morning! We've been playing for eleven hours!

PHIL. I'm sorry, Pinky, but I've got a syndication deadline staring me in the face and I still haven't finished the last panel. How does everybody else keep coming up with punchlines?

ELLIS. Do like "Dennis the Menace" — listen to your kids.

ABBOTT. Do like "Doonesbury" — satirize the politicians.

PINKY. Do like me — steal from "Doonesbury." (*He rips something out of a newspaper.*)

ELLIS. Phil, why don't you do what Sam here does — use the same punchline at the end of every strip — "So what else is new?!"

SAM. Sorry, that one's taken.

PHIL. Okay, we'll play once around, to give Pinky a chance to get even.

ELLIS. Sam, we're playing cards.

SAM. If you don't mind, I want to catch Tess Harding. Those commentaries she does are the brightest thing on the air. (*He turns on the TV set. As he does, lights come up in the TV studio. CHIP is smiling and "talking"—his lips move but there's no sound. He is doing a pet food commercial.*)

PINKY. I can't stand it when the sound's off—I keep thinking they're talking about me. (*He turns the sound on. CHIP is immediately audible.*)

CHIP. —and now for our regular visit to Tess' Corner for her usual no-holds-barred commentary on subjects of—(*Now PHIL clicks off both the picture and sound—the lights go off in the studio.*)

PHIL. I don't want to hear Tess Harding. She's always right! I *hate* people who are always right!

SAM. (*He glances at PINKY.*) It's too bad we're missing her. Who knows, maybe she's talking about Pinky. (*Suddenly, PINKY turns on the set. And, again, the studio lights come up. TESS is just beginning her commentary.*)

TESS. —At the risk of sounding un-American, I'm getting sick and tired of the funnies. Oh, they're all right in their place, I suppose, on the back pages of our daily newspapers, but when this seemingly endless parade of mindless little furry things move out of the barnyard and start invading our art museums, then it's time to call out the marines, round them all up and send them back where they belong, back to the funny papers—

ELLIS. How do you like that dame?

TESS. —How did they ever escape in the first place? —Are we avoiding reality? Are we reverting to childhood? —

PHIL. It all started when we gave them the vote.

TESS. —Whatever the reason, I think the trend is silly and perhaps a little dangerous.

ABBOTT. You're dangerous, lady—

TESS. In short, I'm beginning to see nothing funny about the funnies. Now back to Chip. (*SAM turns off the set and again the studio goes dark. The five men are clearly in total shock.*)

PINKY. What do you know? —she really *was* talking about me.

(*A moment of silence. Then:*)

SAM. Hey, what's wrong with you guys? It's a free country, right? So let's just forget it and play cards.

[MUSIC NO. 3C — FIRST POKER GAME]

(*They sing.*)

"THE POKER GAME"

PHIL.
TWO, PLEASE
  ABBOTT.
I'M PAT.
  PINKY.
I'LL TAKE ONE PLEASE.

SAM. (*spoken*) *Who the hell does she think she is?!!* That lame-brained, over-educated, under-developed moron!! (*He sings.*)
WHO DOES SHE THINK SHE IS
TO THROW SUCH GARBAGE OUT
FIRST THING IN THE MORNING
DOESN'T IT MAKE YOU SICK
TO STOP AND THINK
SOMEWHERE SOME KID
COULD BE WATCHING HER
  PINKY.
WILL YOU THINK OF THAT
  ALL.
SUFF'RING SUCCOTASH!
  PINKY.
I HOPE SHE PAYS
TIT FOR TAT
  ALL.
HOLY MOLEY!
  PINKY.
SHE'LL GET HERS ONE OF THESE DAYS

SAM, PINKY, ABBOTT.	ELLIS, PHIL.
WHO DOES SHE THINK SHE IS	THINK OF THAT
TO THROW SUCH GAR-BAGE OUT	SUFF'RING SUCCOTASH!

FIRST THING IN THE
   MORNING
DOESN'T IT MAKE YOU
   SICK
TO STOP AND THINK
SOMEWHERE SOME KID
COULD BE WATCHING
   HER

I HOPE SHE PAYS

TIT FOR TAT

HOLY MOLEY!
SHE'LL GET HERS
ONE OF THESE DAYS

PHIL.
I'LL SEE YOU
   ELLIS.
THAT BIRD BRAIN
   ABBOTT.
YOU'RE TOO STRONG
   PINKY.
I'M TOO ANGRY TO PLAY
(*spoken*) So.
I'M CALLING IT QUITS, GUYS. GOODBYE
   ELLIS.
ME TOO
I'M SO MAD I COULD DIE

WELL IF YOU'RE GONNA DIE
TAKE THE NEW DRAGON LADY ALONG
   PINKY. (*going*)
'NIGHT, SAM
   ELLIS. (*going*)
SEE YA.
   ABBOTT. (*going*)
'NIGHT, SAM
   PHIL. (*gone*)
'NIGHT, SAM

[MUSIC NO. 3D—FUNNY PAPERS INTRO]

SAM. (*left alone*) Well, Katz old man, she really made a monkey out of us, didn't she? So how'd you like to get even, you mindless little furry thing you—would you like that? Sure you would? (*He goes to his drawing board, turns on the lamp, pulls out a brand new, clean, white sheet of paper, rubs his hands together and picks up a pencil.*) What you clearly need is a playmate—someone you love to hate—someone controversial, abra-

sive, loud-mouthed — in short — (*He sits and starts to draw.*) — a
new cat in town! Opinionated, obnoxious — a real troublemaker.
(*He sings.*)

[MUSIC NO. 4 — "SEE YOU IN THE FUNNY PAPERS"]

"SEE YOU IN THE FUNNY PAPERS"

SAM.
BYE BYE HONEY
SEE YOU IN THE FUNNY PAPERS
SOON

BYE BYE BABY
SEE YOU IN THE FUNNY PAPERS
MAYBE THURSDAY AFTERNOON

OR MAYBE SOONER
LET'S KEEP IT IN DOUBT
IT'S SUCH A SWEET BEGINNING
I WANT TO DRAW IT OUT

SO, THOUGH IT'S
JUST AN OLD EXPRESSION
IT SEEMS APPROPRIATE NOW

SEE YOU IN THE FUNNY PAPERS
ADIO, AUF WIEDERSEHEN, MEOW!

(*spoken*) Okay, now — we'll give her a really big mouth, so she
can put her paw in it — there we go — and teeny-weeny boobs, because she's got so little to get off her chest — beautiful, I hate her
already —

YOUR VOICE AND MANNER
GET UNDER MY SKIN
WE'LL MEET AGAIN, I PROMISE
I'LL PENCIL SOMETHING IN

BUT FOR THE MOMENT
LET'S NOT RUSH IT
THE SWIFT ENTANGLEMENTS END

I'LL SEE YOU IN THE FUNNY PAPERS
YOU'LL BE THERE, DON'T WORRY
MY FRIEND!

(*He pins the completed drawing on his wallboard: Tessie Cat,
    framed in a TV set.*)

SAM. Well, Katz old man, there she is. Now all we need is a
name. How about Alley Cat? No—Sour Puss? No—I got it—
Tessie Cat! Purrfect! (*From* L., *GERALD appears, a tabloid
newspaper in his hand. He reads aloud from it.*)
    GERALD. Katz is eating his morning cereal in front of his tele-
vision set. He is watching—Tessie Cat?—(*SAM laughs.*)—who
says: "Dear viewers—how will you ever amount to anything if
you don't stop wasting time with low-brow pursuits like television and start doing something worthwhile with your lives. I
mean, you're never going to become rich and famous like me sitting home and watching stupid shows like this one"—(*SAM
laughs.*) And Katz says, "So what else is new?" (*a beat*) Incredible. (*He walks into the new set which has moved on.*)

SCENE 3

*TESS' office: consisting of an outer, secretary's (GERALD's)
    office, and TESS' private one.*
AT RISE: *GERALD crosses to his desk, still studying the tabloid
    newspaper he is reading.*

GERALD. Tessie Cat. I don't believe it. (*The phone rings and
he answers it.*) Miss Harding's office—No, she's not in at the
moment, who's calling?—Oh, I'm so sorry, senator, I didn't
recognize your voice. How are things in Washington?—No, of
course we wouldn't mind if you called collect from now on—The
comic strip? No, I'm positive she hasn't seen that yet. No, she
couldn't have, senator, she's been at the Indian Consulate all
afternoon interviewing Mother Teresa—It's her first television
interview since she won the Nobel Peace Prize—No, I meant
Mother Teresa. Miss Harding hasn't won it. Yet—(*He turns to
the door.*) Hold on, senator, I think I hear her—(*He quickly
hides the newspaper. Then TESS enters, all business.*)
    TESS. Get Larry for me in Colorado. And hold all calls.
(*Without stopping she sails through, into her own office.*)

GERALD. (*into the phone*) She saw it, senator. We'll have to get back. (*He disconnects, then starts dialing a number, area code first. In her office, TESS is clearly agitated as she paces, waiting for GERALD to get her call.*) It's ringing! (*In TESS' office, she picks up the phone.*)

TESS. Larry? — Larry *darling,* how are you, it's good to hear your voice — How's Jane? — Your wife, Jane — All right, Jan. For one lousy letter you're not going to sulk, are you? Larry, you're in the newspaper business — I was wondering if you happened to know anything about a certain, obscure cartoonist named — Oh, you saw it, too. My God, everybody in the whole world must've seen it! Would you believe Mother Teresa saw it? — Tell me the truth, Larry, you didn't find it particularly, well, funny, did you? — That's always been your most glaring fault, Larry, a very weird sense of humor. I'm just glad we're not married any more — No, of course I didn't mean it. I adore you, you know that — Goodbye, darling, love to Jane! (*She hangs up. Thinks for a moment, then goes to GERALD's desk.*) You saw it too, right?

GERALD. Right.

TESS. Gerald, who is this character? What's he got against me, anyway?

GERALD. He's a cartoonist. Obviously he's a trifle upset about that editorial you did.

TESS. Why? What'd I say?

GERALD. Weren't you listening?

TESS. Of course I was. And I was absolutely right. (*She notices a basketful of letters on her desk.*) What's all this?

GERALD. You wouldn't think there were that many cartoonists in the entire country, would you?

TESS. Gerald, you've been with me a long time — you know that in this business, decisions have to be made quickly, on hunches sometimes, but in the long run, I think my record speaks for itself — I think I can look back and safely say — (*She sings.*)

[MUSIC NO. 5 — "WHEN YOU'RE RIGHT, YOU'RE RIGHT"]

"WHEN YOU'RE RIGHT, YOU'RE RIGHT"

TESS.
I WAS RIGHT

GERALD.
THAT'S RIGHT
TESS.
I WAS PERFECTLY RIGHT
GERALD.
RIGHT
TESS.
MY INSTINCTS WERE VALID AND STRONG, RIGHT?
GERALD.
THAT'S RIGHT
TESS.
WHEN YOU'RE RIGHT, YOU'RE RIGHT
GERALD.
RIGHT
TESS.
I KNOW WHEN I'M RIGHT
CAN YOU HONESTLY SAY I WAS WRONG?
GERALD.
RIGHT – UH, WRONG!
TESS.
I WAS RIGHT
GERALD.
RIGHT
TESS.
THAT'S RIGHT
I WAS PERFECTLY RIGHT
GERALD.
RIGHT
TESS.
I WAS AND I'VE BEEN ALL ALONG, RIGHT?
GERALD.
THAT'S RIGHT
TESS.
WHEN YOU'RE RIGHT, YOU'RE RIGHT
GERALD.
RIGHT
TESS.
I KNOW WHEN I'M RIGHT
IT'S REMARKABLY RARE THAT I'M WRONG, RIGHT'
GERALD & TESS.
THAT'S RIGHT!

Tess. (*spoken*) I mean, even in my personal life I've always made the right decisions — (*speaks in rhythm*)
WHEN I MARRIED LARRY
I WAS EIGHTEEN, HE WAS TWENTY
WE WERE BOTH JOURNALISM STUDENTS IN MISSOURI
AND ALL HE WANTED TO BE WAS WILLIAM ALLEN
  WHITE
I HAD A JOB AT THE LOCAL T.V. STATION
I WAS ONLY DOING THE WEATHER BUT SOME
  NETWORK EXECUTIVE
HAPPENED TO SEE ME ONE NIGHT
SO, I KNEW I HAD TO GO TO NEW YORK
AND LARRY WOULD BE HAPPIER EDITING A
  NEWSPAPER IN COLORADO OR SOMEWHERE
SO, IT WAS TIME FOR A BREAK
AND THOUGH WE BOTH STILL CARED FOR EACH
  OTHER
HE HAD TO GO HIS WAY
AND I HAD TO GO MINE
SO, THE SPLIT-UP WAS NOT A MISTAKE!
(*sings*)
LARRY'S REMARRIED AND BLISSFUL OUT WEST
AND I LOVE *MY* CAREER — IT WAS ALL FOR THE BEST!

I WAS RIGHT
  Gerald.
THAT'S RIGHT
  Tess.
I WAS PERFECTLY RIGHT
  Gerald.
RIGHT
  Tess.
MY INSTINCTS WERE VALID AND STRONG, RIGHT?
  Gerald.
THAT'S RIGHT
  Tess.
WHEN YOU'RE RIGHT, YOU'RE RIGHT
  Gerald.
RIGHT
  Tess.
I KNOW WHEN I'M RIGHT

IT'S REMARKABLY RARE WHEN I'M WRONG, RIGHT?
 TESS & GERALD.
THAT'S RIGHT!

 TESS. (*spoken*) And need I even mention my professional life?
When I started doing hard news, *those* decisions weren't easy,
you know—(*speaks in rhythm*)
I REMEMBER INTERVIEWING NASSER
AND TELLING HIM, "LOOK, GAMAL, DO ME A FAVOR
AND DO NOT INVADE ISRAEL!"
BUT NO, NO, HE WENT RIGHT AHEAD
THEN THERE WAS EHRLICHMAN AND HALDEMAN
AND I TOLD THEM, "BOYS, YOU'VE *GOT* TO TELL THE
  TRUTH!"
BUT WHAT DID THEY DO? LIES! LIES! EVERY WORD
  THAT THEY SAID!
AND ALEXI PETRIKOV, THAT RUSSIAN DANCER
SAID HE WAS BORED AT THE BOLSHOI
AND I TOLD HIM, "DEFECT," BUT HE WAS TOO MEEK
NOW, A FRIEND OF MINE
WHO JUST GOT BACK FROM MOSCOW SAYS HE'S
FRUSTRATED, UNHAPPY
AND DANCING "SPARTACUS" FOUR TIMES A WEEK!
(*sings*)
A BRAGGART, I'M NOT
 GERALD.
RIGHT
 TESS.
BUT DOESN'T IT SHOW
MY MARGIN FOR ERROR'S EXCEEDINGLY LOW?

I WAS RIGHT
 GERALD.
THAT'S RIGHT
 TESS.
I WAS PERFECTLY RIGHT
 GERALD.
RIGHT
 TESS.
MY INSTINCTS WERE VALID AND STRONG, RIGHT?
 GERALD.
THAT'S RIGHT
 TESS.
WHEN YOU'RE RIGHT, YOU'RE RIGHT

GERALD.
RIGHT
TESS.
I KNOW WHEN I'M RIGHT
IT'S REMARKABLY RARE WHEN I'M WRONG, RIGHT?
TESS & GERALD.
THAT'S RIGHT!
TESS. (*spoken*) And now we have this second-rate cartoonist.
My God, what's all the uproar about? Obviously I made the right
decision again—(*speaks in rhythm*)
ALL I DID WAS PRESENT A COGENT
WELL-CONSIDERED ANALYSIS
OF HOW THE FUNNIES ARE THRASHING THE ARTS
AND IT SETS OFF THIS RIDICULOUS FLAP—
—SO HE CREATES ME AS A CHARACTER IN HIS
   PUERILE LITTLE STRIP
TO PUT KLUTZ, OR WHATEVER THE HELL THE CAT'S
   NAME IS
ON THE MAP

(*SAM now enters the outer office and stands by the door, un-
   noticed.*)

WELL, WHEN I GET THAT PUBLICITY-GRABBING
EXPLOITIVE, DETESTABLE
LITTLE WEASEL IN HERE, WILL I MAKE HIM SQUIRM!
I BET I CAN TELL YOU WHAT HE LOOKS LIKE, TOO
HE'S PROBABLY A SHORT, NAPOLEONIC,
BALD, PUDGY, PASTY-FACED WORM!
(*Now GERALD notices SAM.*)
   GERALD. Yes?
   SAM. Sam Craig to see Miss Harding.
   GERALD. (*into speaker phone*) Miss Harding, Mr. Sam Craig
is here—
   TESS. Wonderful! Please send Mr. Sam Craig in! (*sings*)
THERE'S ONLY ONE WAY TO TREAT VERMIN LIKE
   THAT
I'LL SHOW HIM WHAT CATS ARE, THAT BEADY-EYED
   RAT—
(*She stops, turns and sees him.*) Mr. Craig—?
   SAM. Look, Miss Harding, I know you saw the newspaper. I
came here to tell you—(*stops*)—You know, you're really better
looking than you are on television—a lot better.

Tess. Mr. Craig, before you say something more, let me tell you something straight out —(*She sings.*)
I WAS WRONG
THAT'S RIGHT
I WAS TOTALLY WRONG—

Gerald. (*from other room*)
NO!

Tess.
—AND NOT TO CONFESS WOULD BE SMALL
THAT'S RIGHT

WHEN YOU'RE WRONG, YOU'RE WRONG, RIGHT?
I KNOW WHEN I'M WRONG
AND YOU'RE NOT WHAT I PICTURED AT ALL

RIGHT!
I WAS BAD
THAT'S RIGHT
AND I MUST HAVE BEEN MAD
BUT MY BARK IS MUCH WORSE THAN MY BITE

Sam.
IS THAT RIGHT?

Tess.
SO LET'S COOL IT, LET'S
I ACKNOWLEDGE MY DEBTS—
(*spoken*) *I* know!
CAN I BUY YOU DINNER TONIGHT?

Sam.
ALL RIGHT—

Tess. Terrific! What are we waiting for?

(*As the music swells, they head out into the street, past a protesting GERALD, as a street drop comes in.*)

Gerald. Miss Harding—you're not actually leaving now, are you?

(*on the street*)

Tess.
AS I'VE SAID ALL ALONG
ALL MY INSTINCTS ARE STRONG

WHEN I SAID, "I WAS WRONG"
I WAS RIGHT!
(*spoken*) Right?
    SAM.
RIGHT
    BOTH.
THAT'S RIGHT!
(*After song:*)

[MUSIC NO. 5A — RIGHT PLAYOFF]

SAM. It's a little early for dinner, you know — how about if I took you somewhere first?

TESS. What did you have in mind?

SAM. My place.

TESS. (*She stops.*) Mr. Craig, call me old-fashioned, but first comes "How do you do." *Then* comes your place.

SAM. I meant my studio, where I work.

TESS. Oh. (*The street drop goes out, revealing SAM's studio.*)

SAM. Because I don't think you know a damn thing about what you call "the funnies." (*They have entered his studio.*)

SCENE 4

SAM's studio.
AT RISE: *As SAM and TESS enter.*

TESS. Yeah? What makes you think so?

SAM. You call them "the funnies." It's condescending — like my calling your racket "the idiot tube." That commentary you did — it was downright ignorant. Want to hear why?

TESS. No thanks.

SAM. Okay, I'll tell you. You didn't do your homework. Shame on you, lady, you're better than that! Here, you want to learn something? We've got our own, entire encyclopedia — (*He picks up a large, weighty tome.*) — Look through it, I think you'll find that for actual wit, artistry and invention, we've been batting a helluva lot higher than television. (*He hands her the book.*)

TESS. — "Cartoons" —

SAM. From the Italian "cartone," meaning pasteboard. Did

you know that Leonardo drew cartoons? And Hogarth, Goya, Toulouse-Lautrec, Daumier—

TESS. —Not to mention Sam Craig—

SAM. Yeah, him, too. It's all in there.

TESS. (*thumbing through it*) Tell me, how does a relatively sane person go about becoming a cartoonist, anyway?

SAM. With me it was pretty simple—it's all I ever knew how to do. As a kid I always liked to doodle, and damned if the things I drew didn't look a lot like the things I was drawing. After school, I headed out west, to the great white father: Uncle Walt and his magical, mystical mouse factory. From there, I got a job as a background man for Tarzan.

TESS. You drew Tarzan?

SAM. No, only the backgrounds. From there I became the lettering man ·for Steve Canyon. You know, only the letters— POW!—BLAM!—GULP!

TESS. (*always the reporter*) Wait, I want to get that down— (*She grabs a pen from his table.*)

SAM. (*taking it away*) Hey, not with that! That has a number four nib! We happen to be very strange about our pens. We go crazy if anybody else touches them. I used to use an old Speedball—but now I've switched to this hot little Japanese number.

TESS. So what else is new?—(*examines the stuffed figure of KATZ*) And Katz, where did he come from.

SAM. Oh, Katz, I got the idea for him on the subway. I looked around and there he was—everywhere. A middle-class working cat, trying to make it in the big city. And, like all New Yorkers, nothing surprises him: Martians just landed in Central Park and got mugged? So what else is new?

TESS. He sounds Jewish.

SAM. Everyone in New York sounds Jewish. Even the Puerto Ricans. (*Spanish accent*) "Hey man, don't be such a schmuck!"

TESS. (*laughing*) Tell me, why isn't he married?

SAM. He was. Once upon a time.

TESS. What happened to her?

SAM. She ran off with a Siamese.

TESS. Oh, that explains it.

SAM. Explains what?

TESS. His hostility towards women. Your furry friend gave it to me pretty good today.

SAM. You hit us first.

TESS. Is that why you came up to my office?

SAM. I came up to apologize. I figured that maybe I'd been a bit too rough and I could see where you might be upset —

TESS. Upset? Don't be silly. Why should I be upset, you shit?

SAM. Oh, good. For a minute there I thought you might be upset. Look, I'm trying to apologize. Why don't we kiss and make up?

TESS. I'll kiss, but I don't know about making up.

SAM. Good. (*He considers what she's said, then reaches out for her — but a loud beeping sound begins and he jumps.*) My God, you're booby-trapped!

TESS. It's only Gerald — (*She reaches into her bag and pulls out a paging device, the sort doctors use, and switches it off.*)

SAM. (*He takes it from her and examines it.*) Why do you call it Gerald?

TESS. No, Gerald's my secretary. Mind if I use your phone? (*She has picked up the receiver and punches out a number before he can answer.*)

SAM. No, go right ahead.

TESS. (*into phone*) Gerald, what's up — You're kidding! Is it official? — That's terrific! Get in touch with the management right away and book him for the show. Call me back, the number here is — (*She checks the number.*) — Dagwood?

SAM. 324-9663 — just dial Dagwood.

TESS. — Just dial Dagwood — *Dagwood,* like in the funny — like in the cartoon. (*She hangs up.*)

SAM. Well come on, what's so exciting?

TESS. Alexi Petrikov, one of the hottest dancers in the world, is coming to New York with the Bolshoi next month. I did a wonderful show with him when I was in Moscow last year. Afterward, we were having dinner alone in his apartment and I asked him if he didn't want to defect. But I think he misunderstood. (*The phone rings and TESS answers it.*) Gerald — Yes, I know he's in New York — You mean right now? — All right, what's his number? — (*She grabs a pen from the work table. He slaps her hand and gives her another one.*) — Yeah — I got it — What? — I don't have to sign those tonight, do I? — All right, bring them by — (*to SAM*) Would you give Gerald an address?

SAM. (*taking the phone*) Four score and seven years ago —

TESS. Come on —

SAM. (*resigned*) 210 Bank Street. — Got that, Gerald? — Goodbye. (*He hangs up.*)

TESS. I'm sorry, but Bjorn Borg's flying back to Sweden tonight. It'll only take a minute. (*She starts dialing.*) You don't mind, do you?

SAM. Please, it's a privilege for me merely to be present.

TESS. (*into the phone*) Mr. Borg, please—Tess Harding. (*to SAM, while waiting*) My life really isn't like this all the time—usually it's much more—(*into the phone*) Bjorn!—(*in Swedish*) God afton, min van, hur mar du? ("Good afternoon, my friend, how are you?") Is retirement agreeing with you?—I told you there was more to life than topspin—Yeah—Yeah—Yeah—

[MUSIC NO. 5B—NAP TIME]

(*The scene blacks out for a moment, except for the light on SAM as he settles in and falls asleep. Then, the lights come back on. TESS is still on the phone, but GERALD is now present, sitting beside her, placing letters for her to sign in front of her.*)

TESS. —Yeah—Yeah—Yeah—So tell me, Placido—how are the concerts going in South America?—Well, do you think it was wise to sing "There'll Always Be An England" in Buenos Aires?—

SAM. (*raising his head*) Is it morning yet?

TESS. —I've got to go now, Placido. When you get back to New York be sure to call. Goodbye, Placido—I'm sorry, Pla*th*ido—adi*oth,* Pla*th*ido—thee you thoon.

SAM. What time is it, anyway?

GERALD. Seven twenty-one.

SAM. Oh, hi, Gerald. (*to TESS*) I just had the most horrible nightmare—I dreamt I got my phone bill.

TESS. Stop worrying, I used a credit card. (*She has returned to signing the letters which GERALD continues to place in front of her.*)

SAM. Do you realize you were on the phone for two full hours? You must've talked to everybody but the Pope.

GERALD. That reminds me. There was a call from Jean-Paul—

SAM. I don't believe it—

GERALD. —Jean-Paul Belmondo. He can do the show in September.

TESS. Terrific. Make sure we book him for the second half, though. He likes to sleep late. (*She remembers and giggles.*)

SAM. Ms. Harding, if I remember correctly you were going to buy me dinner.

TESS. Oh God, you're right. Gerald, call Pearl's.

SAM. What's Pearl's?

GERALD. You must be joking.

TESS. A marvelous Chinese restaurant. Gerald, tell them we'll be there in —

SAM. Hey, I can do it, okay? *I can do that!* (*He takes the phone, dials 411.*) Hello, information? — The number for Pearl's Restaurant —

GERALD. 586-1060.

SAM. You're quite a pearl yourself, Gerald. (*He dials.*) Half an hour all right?

GERALD. Fine.

SAM. Are you coming, too, Gerald?

GERALD. Chinese food gives me headaches.

SAM. That's too bad. (*into the phone*) Hello, Pearl's? I'd like a table in thirty minutes, please, the name is Sam Craig — Nothing at all? — (*to TESS*) They don't seem to have any —

TESS. Here, I'll do it — (*She takes the phone.*) Pearl? — Hello, Pearl, dear, it's Tess Harding — (*in Chinese*) Ngor scheung deng leung gor yun toy — ("I want to reserve a table for two.") Thanks, Pearl, you're an angel. (*She hands SAM back the phone and returns to GERALD and the last few letters. SAM is both impressed and annoyed.*) All right, Gerald, you know where we'll be if anything really urgent comes up, which I hope it won't.

SAM. I'm not going. (*TESS and GERALD stop and turn to him.*)

TESS. What did you say?

SAM. I'm not going.

TESS. Why not?

SAM. I don't want to.

GERALD. What are we going to say to Pearl?

SAM. Just tell her — (*fake Chinese*) — Cow dung chow fon cooey!

TESS. (*laughs*) Got that, Gerald? And while you're at it, call Elaine's.

SAM. I'm not going.

TESS. Or better yet, make it Patsy's.

SAM. Don't you ever listen, lady? I don't want to go to Elaine's, Patsy's, Jilly's, Sardi's, Wally's, or even Maxwell's Plums.

TESS. Where *do* you want to go?

SAM. Nowhere. Not tonight. Tonight got off on the wrong foot — yours.

TESS. Don't tell me you're one of those men who feels threatened if he's not in charge —

SAM. No, no, you can be in charge, I just want to be included in the conversation.

TESS. (*studies him*) Well, I guess I did screw things up, I'm sorry. Sure you won't reconsider tonight?

SAM. Absolutely not. But I'll tell you what — I'll take *you* to dinner Monday night, just the two of us.

TESS. Okay, it's a deal.

GERALD. (*who has consulted an agenda*) Uh, uh, no good.

TESS. What do you mean?

GERALD. You're debating Phyllis Schafly — does a career woman have time for normal social life.

TESS. Oh damn, I forgot. Sorry, Sam. I'm afraid Monday's out.

[MUSIC NO. 6 — "SHUT UP, GERALD"]

(*They sing:*)

"SHUT UP, GERALD"

SAM.
HOW ABOUT TUESDAY?
GERALD.
THAT'S IMPOSSIBLE
SAM.
SHUT UP, GERALD
TUESDAY IT IS, THEN
HOW ABOUT THURSDAY?
GERALD.
E.L. DOCTOROW
SAM.
SHUT UP, GERALD
THURSDAY IT IS, THEN
TUESDAY AND THURSDAY
AND MONDAY THE FOLLOWING WEEK?
GERALD.
DRINKS WITH TEDDY

TESS.
WHAT?
GERALD.
YOU'VE CANCELLED TWICE ALREADY
TESS. Oh.
SHUT UP, GERALD
MONDAY IT IS, THEN
AND HOW ABOUT FRIDAY?
(*GERALD remains silent, but mimes "No."*)
SHUT UP, GERALD
GERALD.
I DIDN'T SAY ANYTHING!
BOTH.
TUESDAY AND THURSDAY
AND MONDAY AND FRIDAY
EACH AN UNBREAKABLE DATE
STARTING NEXT TUESDAY AT EIGHT
TESS.
THEN WHAT?
SAM.
THEN WHAT?
TESS.
WHAT THEN?
SAM.
WHAT THEN?
WAIT!

(*TESS and GERALD start to leave. TESS and SAM continue to look at one another.*)

TESS. 'Bye.
SAM. 'Bye.
GERALD.
REALLY, MISS HARDING
YOU'RE IMPOSSIBLE
SAM & TESS. (*together, their eyes still on each other*)
SHUT UP, GERALD!

(*TESS and GERALD leave. SAM, lost in thought, steps DS. as a screen comes in behind him.*)

SAM. Well, Katz old man, I think we're in a lot of trouble. I mean, just look what you're doing. A week ago, you were trying to strangle her. Now you're making dates. What do you think you're doing? (*He waits for an answer but there is none.*) Hey, Katz—I'm talking to you!—*Katz!!* (*Now the figure of KATZ appears, animated, on the screen.*)

KATZ. What do you want?

SAM. Aren't you the cat who said it wasn't going to happen again?

KATZ. Why don't you mind your own business?

[MUSIC NO. 7 — "SO WHAT ELSE IS NEW?"]

SAM. Look, Katz, she'll walk all over you. She'll have you altered.

KATZ. Stop being so catty! I know what I'm doing.

SAM. No you don't! Remember what you said? Do you remember?—(*He sings:*)

"SO WHAT ELSE IS NEW?"

ONCE YOU VOWED
YOU'D NEVER FALL AGAIN
DISALLOWED
BRAVING THAT SQUALL AGAIN
NOW YOU'RE COWED
GIVING YOUR ALL AGAIN
DUMB!
KATZ.
TRUE!
SO WHAT ELSE IS NEW?
SAM.
ONCE YOU'D SHOUT
WON'T BE DEPRESSED AGAIN
THINK ABOUT
GOING THROUGH EST AGAIN
NOW YOU'RE OUT
BEATING YOUR CHEST AGAIN
TRITE!
KATZ.
TRUE!
SO WHAT ELSE IS NEW?

WOMAN OF THE YEAR

WISE OLD RALPH WALDO EMERSON FINDS
THAT A FOOLISH CONSISTENCY IS
THE HOBGOBLIN OF LITTLE MINDS
RIGHT ON, WALDO!

SAM.
ONCE YOU SWORE
YOU'D NEVER REACH AGAIN
PACE THE FLOOR
SLURRING YOUR SPEECH AGAIN
NOW, ONCE MORE
INTO THE BREECH AGAIN!
TRUE!
KATZ.
WELL SO WHAT?
SAM.
SO WHAT ELSE?
SAM & KATZ. (*together*)
SO WHAT ELSE IS NEW?

SAM. Remember that wife of yours, Katz? A regular pussycat.
Thick, silky orange hair, a soft, purring voice, long, sexy whis-
kers—you were crazy about her. So what did she do? She went
into heat and fell for a peeping tom.
KATZ.
SO WHAT ELSE IS NEW?

SAM. And if that weren't bad enough, *you* were stuck with the
alimony! Ain't *that* the cat's meow! She's living with *him,* but
you're the one who's paying for the litter.
KATZ.
SO WHAT ELSE IS NEW?

SING THE SONG IRA GERSHWIN DESIGNED
WHERE THE MORAL WAS JENNY SHOULD NOT HAVE
    MADE UP HER MIND
AYE, AYE, IRA!
SAM.
ONCE YOU QUIPPED
WON'T BE ENRAPT AGAIN
STAY WELL-ZIPPED
NOT TO BE ZAPPED AGAIN
NOW YOU'RE TRIPPED
TOTALLY TRAPPED AGAIN

(*as he tap-dances*)
TRUE!
    KATZ.
WELL, SO WHAT?
    SAM.
WELL, SO WHAT?
    KATZ.
SO WHAT ELSE?
    SAM.
SO WHAT ELSE?
    SAM & KATZ. (*together*)
SO WHAT ELSE IS NEW?
SO WHAT ELSE IS NEW?
SO WHAT ELSE IS NEW?

    SAM. Watch yourself, Katz—this could be a major cattastrophe! (*As SAM starts off, he suddenly stops—TESS has reentered.*)

[MUSIC NO. 7AA—FIREWORKS INTRO]

    SAM. I thought you'd left.
    TESS. I forgot my gloves.
    SAM. You weren't wearing gloves.
    TESS. I know.

[MUSIC NO. 7A—FIREWORKS]

(*During the pause that follows, the words: "POW! BLAM! GULP!" appear on the screen. And then, as he takes her hand and leads her off, FIREWORKS explode on the screen. Lights out*)

[MUSIC NO. 8A—BAR INTRO]

SCENE 5

The Inkpot—a Third Avenue saloon containing a bar, a row of booths, a pool table, and, on the walls, caricatures of actual cartoonists.

AT RISE: *MAURY, the proprietor, comes out from behind the bar and joins the four cartoonists—PHIL, ELLIS, ABBOTT, and PINKY—who are playing poker at one of the tables.*

MAURY. Where's Sam? How come he couldn't make the game?

ABBOTT. He said he had to work.

PINKY. Yeah, I wonder what she looks like.

PHIL. Well, we know what she doesn't look like—(*He meows like a cat.*)

[MUSIC NO. 8—SECOND POKER GAME]

ELLIS. The nerve of that dame!

ABBOTT. Has she got any idea how much pleasure we bring to the world? (*They sing:*)

"THE POKER GAME" (Reprise)

MAURY.
THERE'S DONDI
DICK TRACY,
AND BLONDIE,
AND DAGWOOD,
AND BATMAN
ELLIS.
TWO, PLEASE,
THE TOONERVILLE TROLLEY
CARTOONIST.
AND TARZAN
AND MAGGIE AND JIGGS
ABBOTT.
I'M PAT
THERE'S GASOLINE ALLEY
RED RYDER,
B.C.
PINKY.
I'LL TAKE ONE PLEASE
BOYS.
DON WINSLOW
AND POGO
THE WIZARD OF ID,
KRAZY KAT,
ANOTHER CARTOONIST.
THINK OF THAT!
ALL.
WILL YOU THINK OF THAT
LEAPIN' LIZARDS!

I HOPE SHE PAYS
TIT FOR TAT.
GLORIOSKY
SHE'LL GET HERS ONE OF THESE DAYS
   PINKY.
WHO DOES SHE THINK SHE IS
TO THROW SUCH GARBAGE OUT
FIRST THING IN THE MORNING
DOESN'T IT MAKE YOU SICK
TO STOP AND THINK
SOMEWHERE SOME KID
COULD BE WATCHING HER

PINKY.	OTHERS.
WHO DOES SHE THINK SHE IS	THINK OF THAT
TO THROW SUCH GARBAGE OUT	SUFF'RING SUCCOTASH!
	HOPE SHE PAYS
FIRST THING IN THE MORNING	
DOESN'T IT MAKE YOU SICK	TIT FOR TAT
TO STOP AND THINK	HOLY MOLEY!
SOMEWHERE SOME KID	AND GETS HERS
COULD BE WATCHING HER	ONE OF THESE DAYS

   PINKY.
I'M OUT, FOLKS
   PHIL.
NOT ME
   ABBOTT.
ME, NEITHER I THINK THAT I'LL STAY
   PHIL.
YEAH, YOU'RE NOT GONNA SCARE ME AWAY
   ELLIS.
YOU CAN GO TAKE YOUR STRAIGHT AND GO SHOVE
IT STRAIGHT UP HER T.V.
   ABBOTT.
AND I'LL TAKE MY FLUSH AND—
   PINKY. (*pouring beer at the bar*) Hi, Sam—

(*After song: SAM has, indeed, entered looking around anxiously; TESS is with him. PINKY continues pouring his beer even though the glass is already full.*)

SAM. Hi, fellas — Fellas, I want you to say hello to Tess Harding. (*silence*)

TESS. (*smiling*) Hello! (*There's a moment of complete silence as the CARTOONISTS register their surprise and disapproval.*)

MAURY. You're a brave person coming here, Miss Harding — after what you said on television —

TESS. (*an uncertain glance at SAM*) Am I?

SAM. Welcome to the Inkpot, a home for wayward cartoonists.

MAURY. What'll it be, Sam, the usual?

SAM. Of course — Tess?

TESS. The usual sounds just swell. (*She turns to look at the CARTOONISTS.*) Don't these gentlemen have names?

SAM. No, I don't think so. Well, what the hell, that one's Pinky Peters —

TESS. Of course — you draw "Cherokee Charlie," don't you? How do you happen to know all those wonderful things about the Indians?

PINKY. (*abashed*) What? Well, that's sort of a long story —

TESS. I'd like to hear it some time.

SAM. And that's Abbott Canfield —

TESS. "Colonel Corn." He's a delightful character.

ABBOTT. (*nonplussed*) Oh. Well. Thanks. (*SAM is amazed by her performance but is clearly enjoying it.*)

ELLIS. (*to TESS*) I'm Ellis McMaster.

TESS. McMaster — let's see — "Friar Duck"? — no, that's your brother. You're "Half Pint."

ELLIS. (*smiling*) That's right.

TESS. Don't tell your brother but your strip is much funnier. And much more relevant, too.

SAM. Last, and certainly least, Phil Whitaker.

TESS. (*regarding him*) Phil Whitaker —

PHIL. Stuck, right?

TESS. Not at all. You draw "La Cucaracha." I was just trying to imagine what sort of a person would come up with a comic strip about a cockroach.

PHIL. I suppose you don't approve.

TESS. On the contrary. Turning the actual symbol of urban poverty and squalor into one of its victims — I think it's brilliant.

PHIL. You do?

TESS. I do.

PHIL. Thank you.

TESS. Gentlemen, I'm afraid I owe you all an apology — for

what has got to be one of the most uninformed editorial statements ever made on television. I hope you'll let me buy you a drink.

ALL FOUR. *Maury*—!! (*As they crowd up to the bar, SAM pulls TESS a few steps away.*)

SAM. Would you mind telling me how you did that? Last night you didn't know "Peanuts" from popcorn.

TESS. Last night I hadn't read your lovely encyclopedia.

SAM. You memorized nine hundred pages? You didn't have time.

TESS. I didn't need time. Your friends' names all had big red X's next to them.

SAM. (*He looks at her, then laughs.*) You're wonderful.

TESS. Of course. Didn't you know?

MAURY. (*joining them with two drinks in shot glasses*) Here you are, Sam—the usual.

SAM. Thanks, Maury. (*He takes them, handing one to TESS.*) Mud in your eye.

TESS. Down the hatch. (*She empties it in one gulp.*)

SAM. (*impressed*) How long you been drinking bourbon straight?

TESS. Ten, maybe twelve seconds.

MAURY. The specialty tonight is corned beef and cabbage. Jules Feiffer discovered the original Dinty Moore recipe in a "Bringing Up Father" from 1926.

SAM. (*taking the bottle from MAURY*) Later, Maury, later. (*He steers her to a table where they sit. TESS empties her glass again.*) Where'd you learn to drink like that?

TESS. From my dad.

SAM. What was he in, the hollow leg business?

TESS. He was a diplomat. With the foreign service. I was born in Bucharest. Then came Belgrade, Sofia and Tirana—mystery, intrigue, all those exotic languages—(*She pours herself a drink.*)

SAM. Don't stop—

TESS. (*downing her drink*) I wouldn't dream of it.

SAM. I meant the story of your life.

TESS. Right. So, I came home, went to college, got a job, got married, got divorced, got three Emmies, two Peabody's and one Pulitzer and lived happily ever after.

SAM. Ah, but did you live happily ever before? (*But PHIL has arrived at the table.*)

PHIL. Excuse me—I have an important announcement to

make: the board of directors — (*notices they are still at the bar*) — the board of directors — (*They cross to PHIL.*) having just met in executive session, has unanimously passed the following resolution — (*lifts his glass*) — Would you raise your glasses, please —

[MUSIC NO. 9 — "ONE OF THE BOYS"]

(*PINKY raises his eye glasses. They sing:*)

"ONE OF THE BOYS"

PHIL.
BY THE POWER INVESTED IN ME BY THE INKPOT
  SALOON
I HEREBY DUB
TESS HARDING —
  ABBOTT. I'll drink to that!
  PHIL.
— OCCASIONALLY KNOWN AS TESSIE CAT —
  SAM. I'll drink to that!
  PHIL.
FORMER SCOURGE OF ALL MANKIND
AS A NEWLY ELECTED MEMBER OF THE GOOD OLD
  GUYS AND —
WELCOME TO THE CLUB
  ALL CARTOONISTS.
COME YE MEN MISOGYNISTIC
WHO REJECT ALL FEMALE PLOYS
TO BE INFORMED
BY MEANS MOST MYSTIC
NOW AND THEN SOME BROAD IS
ONE OF THE BOYS!
  TESS. Thanks, fellas. Wanna wrestle? (*She sings.*)
I'M ONE OF THE GIRLS
WHO'S ONE OF THE BOYS
ENJOYING THE JOKES AND THE SMOKES AND THE
  NOISE

YOU WANNA GO FISHING
WELL, HAND ME A REEL
I MAJORED IN POKER
SO SHUT UP AND DEAL

I'M ONE OF THE GALS
WHO'S ONE OF THE GUYS
HEY, PUT UP YOUR DUKES
AND I'LL BLACKEN YOUR EYES

BEHIND ALL THE GUCCI AND PUCCI AND PEARLS
I'M ONE OF THE BOYS
ALTHOUGH I'M ONE OF THE GIRLS

I'M ONE OF THE DOES
WHO'S ONE OF THE STAGS
I CHUG-A-LUG BREWS
WHEN I LOSE ON THE NAGS

FORGET THE MAX FACTOR
YOU FIND ON MY FACE
FOR BARBERSHOP FOURS
I'M A FABULOUS BASS

I'M ONE OF THE QUEENS
WHO'S ONE OF THE DRONES
JUST HAND ME THE DICE
AND I'LL RATTLE YOUR BONES

IN SPITE OF THE DRESS, THE FINESSE AND THE POISE
I'M ONE OF THE GIRLS
WHO'S REALLY ONE OF THE BOYS

TESS.	CARTOONISTS.
I'M ONE OF THE GIRLS	COME YE
WHO'S ONE OF THE BOYS	MEN
ENJOYING THE JOKES	MISOGYNISTIC
AND THE SMOKES	
AND THE NOISE	
YOU WANNA GO	WHO
FISHING?	
WELL, HAND ME A REEL	DISDAIN ALL
I MAJORED IN POKER	FEMALE
SO SHUT UP AND DEAL	PLOYS
I'M ONE OF THE GALS	TO BE
WHO'S ONE OF THE GUYS	INFORMED BY
HEY, PUT UP YOUR	MEANS
DUKES	MOST

AND I'LL BLACKEN YOUR   MYSTIC
  EYES
IN SPITE OF THE DRESS   NOW AND
THE FINESSE AND THE   THEN
  POISE   SOME
I'M ONE OF THE GIRLS   BROAD IS
WHO'S REALLY
ONE OF THE BOYS   ONE OF THE BOYS
(*dance*)
  ALL.
SHE'S (I'M) ONE OF THE DAMES
WHO'S ONE OF THE KNIGHTS
HER FRIDAY NIGHT TREAT IS
A SEAT FOR THE FIGHTS
  TESS.
I LOVE TO GO STROKE
WITH A VARSITY CREW
YOU WANNA PLAY SNOOKER?
GO CHALK UP YOUR CUE
  ALL.
SHE'S (I'M) ONE OF THE JANES
WHO'S ONE OF THE JOES
  TESS.
HERE, HOLD MY CIGAR
WHILE I POWDER MY NOSE
I'VE LAYERS OF LACQUER A LADY ENJOYS
I'VE EARRINGS AND BRACELETS AND VARIOUS TOYS
BUT I LOVE WHEN I'VE SLIPPED INTO RIPPED
  CORDUROYS
BECAUSE I'M ONE OF THE GIRLS
  BOYS.
ONE OF THE GIRLS
  TESS.
I AM ONE OF THE GIRLS
  BOYS.
ONE OF THE GIRLS
  TESS.
ONE OF THE GIRLS
WHO'S ONE OF THE —
(*spoken*)
Barkeep!!
(*sings*)
BOYS!

Boys.
BOYS!

(*After song: SAM takes TESS' arm.*)

SAM. Excuse me, fellas — Man talk — (*He leads her back to the table.*)

TESS. What's so important?

SAM. Everything — like how you feel about being you.

TESS. I feel very good about it. Always have. I like knowing more about what goes on than most people.

SAM. And telling 'em.

TESS. And telling 'em.

SAM. Then tell me about your husband. Ex-husband.

TESS. Larry? He's in Colorado. Runs a cute little newspaper in a cute little town. Married to a cute little lady named Jane — (*stops, considers*) — Jan. I've never met her. Sweet guy, Larry, a born husband.

SAM. But not yours.

TESS. He wanted a home, a family, a quiet, peaceful life — crazy stuff like that.

SAM. He certainly sounds certifiable. What did *you* want?

TESS. What I've got.

SAM. And that's it?

TESS. The whole story.

SAM. I know, "Film tonight at eleven."

TESS. What about *your* marriage?

SAM. Who said I was married?

TESS. You did.

SAM. I said Katz was married.

TESS. You mean you were never married.

SAM. Yeah, I was married.

TESS. Okay. So what happened?

SAM. She ran off with another guy.

TESS. A Siamese?

SAM. No, an Indian. A first baseman with Cleveland. She caught him off base and threw him out.

TESS. That's a sad story. Calls for another drink. Maury. . . !

SAM. No more drinks. If you're not careful you're going to wind up on the floor.

TESS. Are you serious? I come from a long line of diplomats, mister. Diplomats know how to handle their liquor. You will not find diplomats on a barroom floor. Maury!

SAM. You're not hearing me—

TESS. I hear you, I hear you. Another drink, please.

SAM. (*He sees that MAURY's disappeared. He gets to his feet and heads for the bar.*) Wait here, I'll get it—(*TESS has opened her bag to get her compact.*)

TESS. Jean-Paul was right, you know—

SAM. (*as he goes*) Belmondo—

TESS. Sartre. Life is absurd—(*She drops the contents out of her bag onto the floor.*) Oh, damn—(*as she sits on the floor to retrieve her stuff*)—absolutely ridiculous. And what can you do about it? Not a helluva lot, right?

SAM. Right!—Are you okay?

TESS. Perfectly!—I mean, as Sartre said, and, uh, maybe he didn't even say it first because, uh, maybe it was Heidegger, come to think of it—And who knows, Heidegger probably got it from Kierkegaard because, uh, he was always getting things from Kierkegaard—as which among us has not? Where was I?—(*SAM has arrived back and squats down to hand her another drink.*)

SAM. Are you comfortable?

TESS. You mean sitting on the floor under a table in a saloon? No, I'm not comfortable. (*He puts his arm around her shoulder and she leans back, against his chest.*)

SAM. How's that?

TESS. Extremely comfortable.

SAM. Look, Tess—

TESS. I'm looking, Sam—

SAM. There's something I want to get off my chest.

TESS. (*sitting up*) I'm too heavy—

SAM. No. I just wanted to say—(*TESS' beeper goes off.*) My God, it's the little corporal again! The bastard must have radar!

TESS. I'll turn it off—

SAM. No, let me—(*He takes it from her and drop it into a glass of water where it gurgles and dies.*)

TESS. Poor Gerald—

SAM. Tess, listen to me—How come there aren't a bunch of guys around you that I have to beat off with a baseball bat? I mean, lady, you are something special.

TESS. What?

SAM. Tess, you're not hearing me!

TESS. I hear you, I hear you—

SAM. I want to know why I don't have to stand in line.

TESS. Why?

[MUSIC NO. 10—"TABLE TALK"]

(*She sings:*)

"TABLE TALK"

TESS.
I SCARE THEM AWAY
THE MEN IN MY LIFE—
SAM.
I LOVE YOU
TESS.
I'M SORRY?
SAM.
WHAT WERE YOU SAYING?
TESS.
THE MEN IN MY LIFE

I MAY BE TOO STRONG
I'M TALL FOR MY HEIGHT
SO MAYBE—
SAM.
I LOVE YOU
TESS.
IT'S MY FAULT
SAM.
BUT—
TESS.
LEMME GO ON
SAM.
I'M SORRY
TESS.
'S AW'RIGHT
(*She rises, none too steadily.*)
THEY SEEM TO RETREAT
THE MORE I ADVANCE—
SAM.
I LOVE YOU

Tess.
EXCUSE ME?
     Sam.
FORGET IT
     Tess.
IF ONLY
THEY'D GIVE IT A CHANCE
AND STAND UP, AS THEY SHOULD
     Sam. (*rising*)
I CERTAINLY WOULD
     Tess.
AND SAY, "I LOVE YOU"—
     Sam.
I LOVE YOU
     Tess.
THAT'S IT EXACTLY—

COMPETITIVE MEN
RESENT MY SUCCESS
THE OTHERS—
     Sam.
SAY, TESSIE—
     Tess.
LET'S SEE NOW—
     Sam.
NOW LISTEN
     Tess.
WHERE WAS I?
     Sam.
I LOVE YOU
     Tess.
OH, YES—

MY VIRGINAL CHARMS
HAVE FADED SOMEWHAT—
     Sam.
YOU'RE WONDERFUL
     Tess.
LISTEN—
     Sam.
I LOVE YOU

TESS.
—I GUESS MARIE OSMOND, I'M NOT
BUT ENOUGH ABOUT ME—
    SAM.
HOW MANY FINGERS UP?
(*He is holding up two fingers.*)
    TESS.
THREE
    SAM.
RIGHT. NOW LET'S CHECK YOUR HEARING
    TESS.
WHAT'S WRONG WITH MY HEARING?
    SAM.
I SAID, "I LOVE YOU"
    TESS.
WHAT?
    SAM.
I SAID, "I LOVE YOU"
    TESS.
I HEAR YOU, I HEAR YOU!
(*They kiss as music swells.*)
PLEASE SAY THAT AGAIN
    SAM.
I LOVE YOU
    TESS.
AGAIN, LOUD AND CLEAR
    SAM.
I LOVE YOU!
    TESS. (*Smiling, she snuggles up against him.*)
NOW THAT YOU LOVE ME
ISN'T IT LOVELY RIGHT HERE?

(*As music swells, they begin dancing. As they do:* [MUSIC NO.
    10A — THE WEDDING] *On the screen, KATZ is projected,
    dancing with TESSIE, all animated. Then KATZ proposes
    to TESSIE on one knee, and after she examines the ring
    he gives her under a magnifying glass, she accepts. They
    drive off together in a car, a sign on the back proclaiming
    "JUST MARRIED." Lights out.*)

[MUSIC NO. 10B — FUNNY PAPERS UTILITY]

SCENE 6

TESS' apartment—An elegant living room and bedroom in a co-op on Fifth Avenue, with a terrace, up.
AT RISE: *HELGA, TESS' housekeeper, a solidly built Germanic woman wearing a white uniform enters, carrying a vase of flowers. The phone is ringing.*

HELGA. Ja, ja, ja—hold your God damn horses—(*answers the phone*) Miss Harding's residence—I'm sorry, she is not here now. Can I take the message?—(*writes*) Dinner next Tuesday at your house, ja—Please spell your name—K-I-S-S-I-N—(*Her face lights up.*) Ja, Herr dokter *Kissinger!* Warum haben sie nicht gesacht?—Ja, Dinstag, halb neun—ja—widersehen! (*She hangs up.*) Such a cutie-pie! (*She starts off when the phone rings again.*) Ach du lieber—(*She turns and answers it.*) Miss Harding's residence—No, Miss Harding is not here—I don't know where she is—I said I don't know—Look, mister, when I say I don't know I don't know, but if I *did* know, I still would not tell you! (*hangs up*) Dumm-head. (*She starts off again when the phone rings again.*) I'm going crazy! (*She returns and answers it.*) What is it?!—Oh, is that you, Gerald? I'm sorry, Liebchen, so many people have been calling—What do you mean where is she? You don't know *either?* But that's impossible, Gerald, you *always* know—What do you mean you are worried?—Mr. Craig, the doodle bug? I'm sure she is all right. Since what time is she missing?—*So long?! Mein Gott!* You must call the Polizei! You must call the F.B.E.! You must call the—(*The doorbell rings and she is immediately calm.*) You see? There she is. You always get so excited. Goodbye, Gerald. (*She hangs up and turns in time to see: TESS being carried in, in the arms of TONY the doorman. Behind them comes SAM, carrying a suitcase.*) *Gott in Himmel!* She's been in an accident!
TESS. That's no way to talk about marriage, Helga.
HELGA. Marriage—?
TESS. Mr. Craig wanted to carry me across the threshold but he's got lower back problems.
SAM. Thank you, Tony—I can manage from here.
TESS. (*holding his hand out*) No, thank *you,* Sir. (*SAM shakes it and he goes.*)
TESS. Helga, is there any champagne on ice?
HELGA. Yes, Miss Harding.

TESS. I'm married now, Helga.

HELGA. *Mrs.* Harding.

TESS. No—it's Mrs. *Craig* now.

HELGA. Ja? (*She looks at SAM.*)

SAM. Ja, Helga—we decided to use my name.

TESS. Please take care of Mr. Craig's bag, Helga.

HELGA. (*picking it up*) Where do I put it?

TESS. In my dressing room, of course.

HELGA. You mean he is staying *here?*

SAM. Husbands usually stay with their wives, don't they?

TESS. (*clapping her hands as HELGA glares at SAM*) Schnell, schnell!

HELGA. (*going*) Ja, ja. Schnell. Everything is schnell. Except with the raises.

SAM. Honey, don't you think it would be a good idea if we got one of those big, old apartments on Riverside Drive that could be *our* place?

TESS. But everything is so established here, darling—everyone knows my address, my phone number—

SAM. Yeah, yeah, but I still think—

TESS. Look, I know it's a little strange at first, but as soon as the doorman learns your name you'll feel right at home here, I promise. (*She goes to her desk to rapidly scan her messages.*) Damn—

SAM. What's wrong?

TESS. Alexi Petrikov hasn't called.

SAM. Good.

TESS. Sam! It's very important that I hear from him.

SAM. Yeah, but not tonight, okay? I've made other plans for tonight.

TESS. (*regards him, then smiles*) You're right, I'm sorry. Just force of habit.

SAM. (*puts his arms around her*) Do you suppose I could interest you in some new habits?

TESS. I'm sure you could. (*They kiss. HELGA returns, briskly.*)

HELGA. I make room in the closet.

TESS. Thank you, Helga. We'll take care of everything ourselves. In fact, I'll go get the champagne right now. (*She goes.*)

SAM. Why don't you take the night off, Helga? (*He finds himself at the desk where he picks up TESS' messages.*)

HELGA. (*who has remained, glaring*) Miss Harding does not like anyone fooling around with her desk.

SAM. I'm not fooling around with her —

HELGA. You must not lose anything —

SAM. I won't lose anything! Helga, why don't you take the night off? (*TESS returns carrying a bottle of champagne. HELGA still doesn't move.*) Good night, Helga. (*She stands her ground.*)

TESS. Good night, Helga.

HELGA. Good night, Mrs. (*She heads out.*) Doodlebug.

TESS. You mustn't mind Helga — she's been with me for ages. I think she needs a vacation, though — so she can go home and visit her family.

SAM. In Germany?

TESS. No, Argentina. ([MUSIC NO. 11 — "THE TWO OF US"] *She hands him the bottle, then goes to the bar for some glasses.*) Here, husband — make it go pop. (*They sit on the sofa, facing front, as he opens the bottle and pours.*)

SAM. I can't believe it.

TESS. What?

SAM. There's nobody here.

TESS. Except us.

SAM. Except us. (*They sing:*)

"THE TWO OF US"

SAM.
HERE WE ARE
THE TWO OF US
I CAN'T BELIEVE MY EYES
TESS.
HERE WE ARE
THE TWO OF US
NOW, WHAT A NICE SURPRISE
PERHAPS IT'S TIME FOR CRIBBAGE, DEAR
SAM.
OR TIME FOR WHIST INSTEAD
BOTH.
NO, LOOK, IT'S NEARLY SEVEN, DEAR
IT'S TIME FOR BED —
(*doorbell*)

SAM. It's nobody *I* know. (*doorbell*) Ignore it.

TESS. Good idea. (*GERALD enters, key in hand.*)

GERALD. My God, *where* have you been?

SAM. He has his own key?

GERALD. I've been calling everywhere?

TESS. I'm sorry, Gerald, but the truth is I was getting—

GERALD. Haven't you heard? Alexi Petrikov has vanished.

TESS. What do you mean, vanished?

GERALD. He walked out of his rehearsal this afternoon and he hasn't been seen since. *You* weren't with him, were you?

TESS. Of course not, I was getting—

GERALD. Here's what the A.P. put out on the wire—(*hands her tear-sheets*)

SAM. (*singing*)
HERE WE ARE
THE THREE OF US
THE THREE OF US ALONE
HERE WE ARE
THE THREE OF US
COMPLETELY ON OUR OWN
THE A AND B AND C OF US
CONSORTING ARM IN ARM
LET'S COUNT NOW: ONE PLUS TWO MAKES THREE OF US
AND THREE'S A CHARM

TESS. It's unbelievable. As soon as there's any word on where he is I want you to call me—

SAM. Tess—

TESS. —as long as it's not tonight. You see, Gerald, this afternoon I got—

(*CHIP enters from front door, in a state of some agitation.*)

CHIP. Tess! Thank God you're here. I don't know what to do— I mean I just don't know what the heck to do!!

SAM. Really? About what? (*CHIP turns and looks at SAM, quizzically.*)

TESS. Oh. Chip Salisbury, this is Sam Craig, my new—

CHIP. Hi there, glad we could get together. Tess, listen—I got an offer from N.B.C.—a biggie—to do the "Today" show. Mucho donero.

TESS. But that's wonderful, Chip. What's your problem?

CHIP. Don't you see? It's all about hair! I'll be sitting between Willard Scott who doesn't have any, and Gene Shalit who's got too goddam much! What am I going to do?

TESS. Look, Chip, can't we talk about this tomorrow? The truth is I just got—(*doorbell*)

SAM. Get that, will you, Chipper old boy? (*As CHIP goes to door, SAM again raises his glass to TESS.*)

GERALD. I'd better get some more bubbly.

SAM. Good idea. (*GERALD goes out, TONY comes in from the front door carrying a large basket of flowers.*)

TONY. These just came for you — I figured you want to have them.

SAM. It's Tony, darling. And look what Tony darling brought.

TESS. Oh, they're lovely.

SAM. How about a drink, Tony?

TONY. I don't know, I'm still on duty.

TESS. Isn't that sweet? They're from Larry. He sends congratulations.

TONY. Here's to Larry.

SAM. Larry?

TESS. My husband. (*realizing*) Late husband. *Ex*-husband.

SAM. How did he know?

TESS. I wired him — to let him know he could stop the alimony.

SAM. (*raising his glass*) To husbands — late, ex and otherwise.

TESS. Let's hear it for otherwise. (*The music up and they sing:*)

SAM & TESS.

HERE WE ARE

THE FIVE OF US

THE FIVE OF US ALONE —

SAM. Everybody — sing!

ALL.

HERE WE ARE

THE FIVE OF US

COMPLETELY ON OUR OWN

THERE'S PRACTICALLY A HIVE OF US

ALL COMFY IN THE COMB

LET'S COUNT NOW: ONE, TWO, THREE, FOUR, FIVE
  OF US

IT'S HOME SWEET HOME.

(*Music under; the doorbell sounds again. TWO MEN — PRESCOTT and GORDON, dressed in gabardine suits — enter.*)

PRESCOTT. My name's Prescott. I'm with the F.B.I. I'm afraid your door was open.

TESS. I'm sorry, Mr. Prescott. I'll try to keep it closed from now on.

PRESCOTT. This is Mr. Gordon.

TESS. Is that all you wanted, Mr. Prescott?

PRESCOTT. What? Oh, no, no. We wanted to talk to you.

TESS. Terrific. We were missing a bass, anyway.

PRESCOTT. We're very concerned about this Alexi Petrikov business. We know that you're an acquaintance of his. We think it's possible that the commies may be trying to pull something— (*Phone rings.*)

TESS. Get that, will you, Gerald, and whoever it is, ask them over.

GERALD. (*answering phone*) Yes? (*covering mouthpiece*) It's Havana. You know who.

PRESCOTT. No, who?

TESS. Down, Mr. Prescott. (*takes phone*) Fidel! Como esta? It's Fidel, darling! Oigame, no tengo mas que una sola—

SAM. Let's hear it for Fidel!

TESS. —cosa que preguntarle—

(*Music up. Led by SAM, everyone but TESS sings:*)

ALL.	TESS. —Si se convoca a una
HERE WE ARE	conferencia Naciones Unidas
THE EIGHT OF US	de urgencia y si los Estados
THE EIGHT OF US ALONE	Unidos desean que se celebre
HERE WE ARE	en la Habana, la apoyara
THE EIGHT OF US	usted?—Fidel, por favor,
COMPLETELY ON OUR	puede, contestarla con un si
OWN	o con un no—

ALL.

YOU MAY SEE ONLY SEVEN HERE

BUT LOGIC WILL ALLOW

THANKS TO THE WONDER OF THE TELEPHONE

WE'RE OCHO NOW!

TESS. (*covering the mouthpiece*) Please, I can't hear—

SAM. Pianissimo—

ALL. (*singing in a whisper*)	TESS. Look, Fidel, there's
HERE WE ARE	a bit of confusion here—well,
THE EIGHT OF US	yes, you did hear singing.
THE EIGHT OF US ALONE	You see, it's my wedding
HERE WE ARE	night—I'm married—
THE EIGHT OF US	
COMPLETELY ON OUR	
OWN—	

(*Everyone stops singing upon hearing the news.*)

GERALD. Married—?

ALL. Married—?

SAM. Married—?

TESS. (*into the phone*)—What's that, Fidel? Well, if you really want to, go ahead—(*She holds the phone out and we hear FIDEL singing.*)

ALL.	FIDEL.
—YOU MAY SEE ONLY SEVEN HERE	CONGRATULACIONES
BUT LOGIC WILL ALLOW	QUERIDA, ESTOY MUY CONTENTO
THANKS TO THE WON-DER OF THE TELE-PHONE	POR TI PE BESEO MUCHO ANNOS DE VIDA—CIAO
WE'RE OCHO NOW	

(*Doorbell rings followed by FIVE NEIGHBORS who enter.*)

DANCING COUPLE. It's a party! Hi, everyone!

HELGA. We were having dinner next door, and decided to finish in here.

NEIGHBOR 1. Is it true, Miss Harding? Are you really married?

NEIGHBOR 2. Congratulations, Miss Harding—We think it's just *grand!*

SAM. (*conducting everyone*) All together now, one, two—

HELGA. (*in German*)—drei, vier, funf—

ALL. (*singing*)

HERE WE ARE

THIRTEEN OF US

THIRTEEN OF US ALONE

HERE WE ARE

THIRTEEN OF US

COMPLETELY ON OUR OWN

TESS & SAM.

IT MAY NOT SEEM SERENE OF US

BUT BE PREPARED TO DUCK

ALL.

BECAUSE THERE'S NOW THIRTEEN OF US

AND THAT'S BAD LUCK

(*Everyone dissolves into laughter as they surround the happy couple. SAM and TESS turn to one another and he kisses her. There are "Oh's and Ah's."*)

TONY. Hey! What's the matter with us? These two newlyweds want to be alone. C'mon, everybody, the party's over — let's get out of here — (*They all head for the front door.*)

OTHERS. Yes — goodnight — congratulations — thanks for the drinks — (etc) — (*And they're gone. TESS and SAM are alone. There's a moment of silence finally. They sing:*)

TESS & SAM.
HERE WE ARE
THE TWO OF US
COMPLETELY ON OUR OWN
TESS.
HERE WE ARE
WITH ONE OF US
WHO HATES TO SLEEP ALONE
SAM.
THAT SQUALLING, SPRAWLING CREW OF US
OUR HUGE SUPPORTING CAST
BOTH.
HAS LEFT THE BRAND NEW TWO OF US
TESS.
MY GROOM —
SAM.
MY BRIDE —
BOTH.
ALONE AT —

(*Suddenly, in through the open terrace door springs ALEXI PETRIKOV, a handsome young Slavic ballet dancer, dressed in his practice clothes.*)

ALEXI. Tessitchka!

TESS. Alexi! ("Aleksýay")

SAM. Jesus Christ!

ALEXI. Tess! — (*in Russian*) Máya láhstahchka! Radnáya mayá! ("My swallow! My dearest!" He kisses her.)

SAM. Hey, hey, just one minute!

TESS. It's all right, Sam — it's Alexi Petrikov.

SAM. Oh, good. For a minute I thought it was G. Gordon Liddy.

TESS. (*to ALEXI in Russian*) Alexi, shtaw tea toot dyelayesh? ("What've you been up to?")

ALEXI. (*in Russian*) Ya pyerebyéschik.

TESS. Sam!

SAM. What?

ALEXI. Tea yedýinstvenaya kahmoo ya mahgoo dawvyerýahts. Ya dolshen ahstáhtsah zdyess s'tahbóy. ("I'm a defector. You're the only one I can trust. I must stay here with you.")

TESS. Sam, he defected! He says this is the only place he can stay that's safe.

SAM. Safe? Here? Doesn't he know I'm about to strangle him?

ALEXI. Ktaw éhta? ("Who's that?")

TESS. (*in Russian*) Moi moozh. Me seevódnya puhzheneeléess. ("My husband. Today we were married.")

ALEXI. (*in Russian*) Seevódya? *Moozh?!* Zamyechatyelnaw! ("Today? *Husband?!* Wonderful!" *He grins, broadly leaps over to SAM and kisses him on the mouth.*) Moozh!! ("Husband")

SAM. (*extricating himself*) If someone had told me I'd spend my wedding night kissing a big Russian guy —

TESS. I'm afraid he'll have to sleep here on the sofa. (*to ALEXI, in Russian*) Tsibýeh bóodyet oodáwbnaw spahts toot? ("Will you be comfortable sleeping here?" *She indicates the sofa.*)

ALEXI. (*in Russian*) Da, da. Prehkráhstnaw! ("Yes, yes, perfect!" *He sits on the sofa, trying it out.*)

SAM. (*to ALEXI*) Da, da, maybe you'd like *me* to sleep there — ?

TESS. He only speaks Russian, Sam. *Don't you speak any Russian at all?!*

SAM. No, only a little broken English.

TESS. Just think of it, Sam — two superpowers scouring the city for him and we've got him right here! What a scoop! Isn't this the most exciting thing that ever happened?

SAM. Yeah. I'm all goose pimples. Well. It's getting late. What say we get ready for bed?

TESS. Sam, why don't you go ahead, I've just got a few questions I want to ask Alexi. I'd better go make some coffee. (*She goes off, toward the kitchen.*)

SAM. Tess — *wait* — —

[MUSIC NO. 11A — "THE TWO OF US" — REPRISE]

(*SAM looks at ALEXI who smiles back at him. Then he fetches the bottle of champagne and two glasses, goes to the sofa, sits down beside the RUSSIAN, and sings:*)

HERE WE ARE
THE TWO OF US
I CAN'T BELIEVE MY EYES—

(*He begins whistling the rest of the song, pouring champagne for himself and ALEXI, but he freezes as the RUSSIAN puts a friendly arm around his shoulder. The living room section moves off.*)

[MUSIC NO. 12—"IT ISN'T WORKING"]

SCENE 7

Around New York.
AT RISE: *The CARTOONISTS appear, playing poker—ELLIS, ABBOTT, PINKY and PHIL, with OTHER CARTOON-ISTS around.*

PHIL. Two please.
ABBOTT. I'm pat.
ELLIS. One.
PINKY. Dealer takes three. (*Phone rings.*)
PINKY. —No, no, Sam, of course we understand. You have to be in bed by nine because she gets up at three-thirty every morning. Besides, who wants to play poker after only two months of marriage? You're the luckiest slob on earth, Sam, goodbye. (*He hangs up.*) I've never heard him sound happier. And you know what that means—(*He sings:*)

"IT ISN'T WORKING"

PHIL.
IT ISN'T WORKING
IT ISN'T WORKING
I HATE TO TELL YOU
IT ISN'T WORKING
I KNEW THE MINUTE
I GOT THE CALL
THAT IT ISN'T WORKING

AT ALL!

IT ISN'T WORKING

IT ISN'T WORKING

I'LL BET YOU FIFTY

IT ISN'T WORKING

HE DIDN'T SAY SO

BUT I COULD TELL
ALL CARTOONISTS.
THAT IT ISN'T WORKING SO WELL
PINKY.
AND LATELY HE LOOKS
LIKE A MILLION
DOLLARS
GETS YOU TO SMELLIN'
A RAT
ELLIS.
LATELY THE STRIP HAS
BEEN TWICE AS
FUNNY
WHAT COULD BE
CLEARER THAN THAT?

ELLIS, PINKY, ABBOTT.
IT ISN'T WORKING

IT ISN'T WORKING
ABBOTT.
I BET YOU FIFTY
ELLIS, PINKY, ABBOTT.
IT ISN'T WORKING

HE DIDN'T SAY SO

BUT I COULD TELL

BOYS.
IT ISN'T WORKING
IT ISN'T WORKING

I HATE TO TELL YOU
IT ISN'T WORKING

I KNEW THE MINUTE
I GOT THE CALL

THAT IT ISN'T WORKING
AT ALL

PHIL, ELLIS.	PINKY, ABBOTT.	BOYS.
IT ISN'T WORKING	AND LATELY HE LOOKS	IT ISN'T WORKING
IT ISN'T WORKING	LIKE A MILLION DOLLARS	IT ISN'T WORKING
I HATE TO TELL YOU	GETS YA TO SMELLIN'	I HATE TO TELL YOU
IT ISN'T WORKING	A RAT	IT ISN'T WORKING
I KNEW THE MINUTE	LATELY THE STRIP HAS BEEN	HE DIDN'T SAY SO
I GOT THE CALL	TWICE AS FUNNY	BUT I COULD TELL

THAT IT ISN'T	WHAT COULD	THAT IT ISN'T
WORKING AT	BE CLEARER	WORKING SO
ALL	THAN THAT?	WELL

(*Lights up on CHIP, at his anchor desk.*)

CHIP. — For "Early Bird" this is Chip Salisbury. Join us again on Monday when our guests will be Alexander Solzhenitzyn and Pia Zadora. And I'm happy to report that Tess Harding is back from her belated honeymoon, which she combined with a special assignment in North Korea. After three months of marriage I've never seen her looking happier. Good morning and have a pleasant weekend.

(*The bright TV lights go off, he loosens his tie and sings:*)

CHIP.
IT ISN'T WORKING

    BOYS.
    IT ISN'T WORKING

IT ISN'T WORKING

    IT ISN'T WORKING

I GOT A FEELING

    I GOT A FEELING

IT ISN'T WORKING

    IT ISN'T WORKING

HER LOOK OF RAPTURE,

    HER LOOK OF RAPTURE,

HER GIRLISH GLEE

    ALL.   HER GIRLISH GLEE
SAYS IT ISN'T WORKING TO ME

CHIP.	BOYS.	CARTOONIST.
IT ISN'T		IT ISN'T
WORKING		WORKING
	IT ISN'T	IT ISN'T
	WORKING	WORKING
IT ISN'T		IT ISN'T
WORKING		WORKING
	IT ISN'T	IT ISN'T
	WORKING	WORKING
I GOT AN		IT ISN'T
INSTINCT		WORKING

	I GOT AN INSTINCT	IT ISN'T WORKING
IT ISN'T WORKING		IT ISN'T WORKING
	IT ISN'T WORKING	IT ISN'T WORKING
SHE'S SUCH AN ANGEL		IT ISN'T WORKING
	SHE'S SUCH AN ANGEL	IT ISN'T WORKING
AROUND THE SHOW		IT ISN'T WORKING
	AROUND THE SHOW	IT ISN'T WORKING
		IT ISN'T WORKING
THAT IT ISN'T WORKING I KNOW	THAT IT ISN'T WORKING I KNOW	THAT IT ISN'T WORKING I KNOW

(*Lights up on HELGA, busy doing the laundry, standing between TWO HOUSEKEEPERS, also in uniform, and several NEIGHBORS.*)

HOUSEKEEPERS. (*entering*)
SH BOOM BOOM BOOM BOOM
BOOM BAH BEE AH
SH BOOM BOOM BOOM BOOM
BOOM

HELGA. — You should see my missus and her mister — it's a match made in Himmel! All day long it's hugging and kissing! Four months already, and they *still* can't keep their hands off each other. (*sings*)
IT ISN'T WORKING
IT ISN'T WORKING
WHO KNOWS THEM BETTER?
IT ISN'T WORKING
THEY LOCK THE BEDROOM
THEY NEVER FIGHT
NO, IT ISN'T WORKING,
ALL RIGHT!

GIRLS. (*shout*) It isn't working!

HELGA.
I CAN REMEMBER WHEN
  SHE WAS SINGLE
SHE COULD BE GROUCHY

AND GRIM
NOW EVERY MORNING
  IT'S "HELLO, HELGA"

SHE'S GOT A PROBLEM
  WITH HIM

GIRLS.
IT ISN'T WORKING
IT ISN'T WORKING
WHO KNOWS THEM
  BETTER?
IT ISN'T WORKING
THEY LOCK THE
  BEDROOM, THEY
  NEVER FIGHT
NO, IT ISN'T WORKING
  ALL RIGHT!

HELGA.	BOYS.	GIRLS.
IT ISN'T WORKING		I CAN REMEMBER
IT ISN'T WORKING	IT ISN'T WORKING	WHEN SHE WAS SINGLE
WHO KNOWS THEM BETTER?	IT ISN'T WORKING	SHE COULD BE GROUCHY
IT ISN'T WORKING	WHO KNOWS THEM BETTER?	AND GRIM
THEY LOCK THE BED-ROOM	IT ISN'T WORKING	
THEY NEVER FIGHT	THEY LOCK THE BED-ROOM	NOW EVERY MORNING
	THEY NEVER FIGHT	IT'S "HELLO, HELGA"
NO, IT ISN'T WORKING ALL RIGHT!	NO, IT ISN'T WORKING ALL RIGHT!	SHE'S GOT A PROBLEM WITH HIM!

BOYS.	GIRLS.
SH BOOM BOOM BOOM BOOM	SHU BU DEE AH
BOOM AB BEE DAH	IT ISN'T WORKING
SH BOOM BOOM BOOM BOOM	SHU DU BEE AH
SH BOOM BOOM BOOM BOOM	IT ISN'T WORKING

(*GERALD enters from* R. *with telephone, crossing to* L.:)

GERALD. — Miss Harding's office — Oh, hello, Mr. Buchwald.

I'm sorry but Miss Harding isn't here. She's in Barrytown interviewing the Reverend Sun Myung Moon. She said if she wasn't back in three days we should start looking for her in airports — The marriage? Six months of bliss, absolute bliss! — (*He hangs up and sings:*)

HELGA & CHIP. (*answer*)

IT ISN'T WORKING	----
IT ISN'T WORKING	----
I GET A FEELING	----
IT ISN'T WORKING	----
SHE'S JUST AS CHARM- ING AS SHE CAN GET	----

ALL.
NO, IT ISN'T WORKING, I BET!

GERALD.	HELGA & GIRLS. (*answer*)	BOYS.
AND YESTER- DAY MORN- ING	IT ISN'T WORKING	IT ISN'T WORKING
SHE GOT IN EARLY	IT ISN'T WORKING	IT ISN'T WORKING
SPREADING HER CHARM	I GET A FEELING	IT ISN'T WORKING
LIKE THE PLAGUE	IT ISN'T WORKING	IT ISN'T WORKING
ACTING AS THOUGH	SHE'S JUST AS CHARMING	IT ISN'T WORKING
SHE'S IN SEVENTH HEAVEN	AS SHE CAN GET	IT ISN'T WORKING

GERALD. (*solo*)
THERE'S GOT TO BE TROUBLE WITH CRAIG!

GERALD.
(*w/GIRLS
answering*)

IT ISN'T WORKING	BOYS.	CHIP/CART'S.
IT ISN'T WORKING	YESTERDAY MORNING	IT ISN'T WORKING
IT ISN'T WORKING	SHE GOT IN EARLY	IT ISN'T WORKING
I GOT A FEELING	SPREADING HER CHARM	IT ISN'T WORKING

IT ISN'T WORKING	LIKE A PLAGUE	IT ISN'T WORKING
SHE'S JUST AS CHARMING	ACTING AS THOUGH	IT ISN'T WORKING
AS SHE CAN GET	SHE'S IN SEVENTH HEAVEN	IT ISN'T WORKING

ALL.
NO IT ISN'T WORKING
NO IT ISN'T WORKING ANYMORE
IT ISN'T WORKING ANYMORE – "NO MORE"
IT ISN'T WORKING
IT ISN'T WORKING
I GOT AN INSTINCT
IT ISN'T WORKING, NO!!!

GIRLS.	MEN.	OTHERS.
IT ISN'T WORKING	IT ISN'T WORKING	YESTERDAY MORNING
IT ISN'T WORKING	IT ISN'T WORKING	SHE GOT IN EARLY
I GOT A FEELING		SPREADING HER CHARM
	I GOT A FEELING	
IT ISN'T WORKING		LIKE THE PLAGUE
	IT ISN'T WORKING	
I KNEW THE MINUTE		ACTING AS THOUGH
	I KNEW THE MINUTE	
I GOT THE CALL		SHE'S IN SEVENTH HEAVEN
	I GOT THE CALL	

ALL.
NO IT ISN'T WORKING, NO IT ISN'T WORKING – NO!

GROUP 1.	GROUP 2.	GROUP 3.
IT ISN'T WORKING		
	IT ISN'T WORKING	YESTERDAY MORNING
IT ISN'T WORKING		
	IT ISN'T WORKING	SHE GOT IN EARLY
I GOT A FEELING	I GOT A FEELING	SPREADING HER CHARM
IT ISN'T WORKING		
	IT ISN'T WORKING	LIKE THE PLAGUE
I KNEW THE MINUTE		
	I KNEW THE MINUTE	ACTING AS THOUGH
I GOT THE CALL		
	I GOT THE CALL	SHE'S IN SEVENTH HEAVEN
THAT IT ISN'T WORKING	NO IT ISN'T WORKING	IT ISN'T WORKING
IT ISN'T WORKING	NO IT ISN'T WORKING	IT ISN'T WORKING
		IT ISN'T WORKING

ALL.
AT
ALL!!!!!
NOT AT ALL!!!!!
(*After applause:*)

[MUSIC NO. 12A — WORKING PLAYOFF]

ALL. (*as they exit in all directions*)

NO, IT ISN'T WORKING
NO, IT ISN'T WORKING ANYMORE
IT ISN'T WORKING ANYMORE—"NO MORE!"

IT ISN'T WORKING
IT ISN'T WORKING
I GOT AN INSTINCT
IT ISN'T WORKING

IT ISN'T WORKING
IT ISN'T WORKING
IT ISN'T WORKING—

(*The voices fade as the next scene begins.*)

SCENE 8

TESS' apartment, the living room and bedroom.
AT RISE: *TESS is working sitting on the bed, as GERALD sits by the desk.*

GERALD. Anything else?

TESS. Yes, Gerald, make sure you send a dozen roses to Mrs. Gandhi at the Waldorf, but watch the card this time—she hates being called "Indira Dear."

SAM'S VOICE. (*off*) Hello, darling, I'm home—(*He enters.*)

TESS. H'wo, daddy—

SAM. H'wo. (*He bends and kisses her.*)

TESS. I dare you to do that again—(*as he does*) Yummy. Miss me, darling?

SAM. Does Linus miss his blanket?

GERALD. I suppose "Dear Indira" is just as bad—

SAM. Oh, hello, Gerald.

GERALD. Mr. Craig—

TESS. Poor darling, you must be frozen. Would you like a cup of tea?

SAM. Now that would be lovely.

TESS. Would you mind making it yourself? Helga stepped out for a few minutes, and you know how helpless I am in the kitchen.

GERALD. And a cup for me, please. Milk, no sugar.

SAM. (*an annoyed glance at GERALD*) Helga's back—we came up together in the elevator.

TESS. (*calling off*) Helga—a pot of tea, please—?

HELGA'S VOICE. (*off*) Ja, ja—!

TESS. Tell me about your trip. How did the lecture go?

SAM. It wasn't exactly a lecture—the student newspaper at Marquette University is sponsoring a seminar—every week they invite a leading cartoonist to come and talk about—

TESS. (*She has begun writing on a yellow pad.*) It sounds absolutely fascinating.

SAM. What'cha doing?

TESS. I just thought of a lead-in to my piece on the political unrest in Central America. Listen to this: "Here today—Guatemala."

SAM. (*after a beat*) What'd you think of Katz today?

GERALD. I didn't get it.

SAM. I was asking my wife, Gerald—

TESS. Gosh, darling, I haven't had time to read it yet.

SAM. It's only four panels, for chrissakes, what kind of time do you need?

TESS. I only meant—

SAM. (*moving to the bedroom*) There's a chimpanzee at Princeton who reads it in three minutes flat while swinging from a rubber tire!

TESS. (*following*) I said I was sorry, didn't I?

SAM. No, you didn't.

TESS. Well, I am—(*The phone rings. SAM and GERALD in different rooms, pick up the two extensions simultaneously.*)

SAM. I've got it, Gerald! (*into the phone, as GERALD hangs up*) Who's this?—Oh. Just one minute—(*covers the mouthpiece*) Washington—the Undersecretary of State.

TESS. I can't talk to him now—he's a pest.

SAM. (*into the phone*) She can't talk to you now, you're a pest. (*He hangs up and they glare at each other.*)

TESS. Well, you must've had a pretty rotten time, wherever you were.

SAM. It was Milwaukee and I was lonely as hell.

TESS. (*surprised*) Milwaukee? Is that where Marquette is?

SAM. Of course. I told you that.

TESS. Isn't that funny.

SAM. There's nothing funny about Milwaukee. Why, what's so strange?

TESS. I was in Milwaukee yesterday.

SAM. You—you were—you were in—? Why?

TESS. I'm doing a piece on Senator Proxmire.

SAM. How long were you there?

TESS. 'Til about eleven. I caught the late plane back.

SAM. That means we could've had dinner together.

TESS. Well, I suppose so—but it just never occurred to me.

SAM. Why didn't it occur to you? It sure as hell would've occurred to me!

TESS. Why are you making such an issue out of it, darling? It's an amusing coincidence, that's all.

SAM. No, that's *not* all! The point is that you could've called and you didn't.

TESS. I couldn't have called because I didn't know where you were staying. So you see, your whole point's about nothing! (*In the living room, HELGA has entered with a tray of tea things.*)

HELGA. Here's the tea—where are the people?

GERALD. (*who's been listening*) Shhh. (*They settle down to listen together.*)

SAM. The goddam point isn't whether you actually called—the goddam point is that you never even *thought* of it!

TESS. How do you know I didn't?

SAM. You just said you didn't!

TESS. All right, so I didn't. What does that prove?

SAM. It proves that you weren't very anxious to be with me, that's all.

TESS. Okay, that makes us even.

SAM. *Even?!* What the hell's even about it?

TESS. It never occurred to you to call me, either.

SAM. How could I call you? I didn't know you were there!

TESS. You could've called me here!

SAM. I *did* call you here! *There was no goddam answer!*

TESS. *How could I answer? I was in Milwaukee!* (*The phone rings and she snatches it off the hook.*) *What?!!*—Oh, hello, Larry. I'm sorry, I was just in the middle of something—(*a look at SAM*)—No, it's not serious. How are things in Colorado?—What?—No, I haven't seen the newswire, why?—You're kidding—Really?—Yes, that's wonderful—No, yours is the first call I've had—Thanks, Larry, you're an angel. Love to Jane. (*She hangs up.*)

SAM. Now what?

TESS. The National Association of Women's Organizations

has named me Woman of the Year. The presentation is next week, at their annual banquet. (*a beat*) Isn't that something?

SAM. (*quietly*) Congratulations.

TESS. (*She regards him for a moment.*) Would you have voted for me, Sam? (*They continue to stare at one another, then exit. TESS, offstage, says:*) Men, who needs them—?!! (*There is a CRASH!*)

HELGA. Did you hear that, Gerald? It's the beginning of the end, ja?

GERALD. Helga, who was it who predicted this disaster practically from the first moment?

HELGA. You, ja?

GERALD. And who was it who said, "A cat may *look* at a queen, but he'd better not marry her?"

HELGA. Hitler.

GERALD. It was *I,* Helga.

[MUSIC NO. 13—"I TOLD YOU SO"]

(*He sings:*)
A BRAGGART I'M NOT—
BUT DOESN'T IT SHOW?
MY MARGIN FOR ERROR IS EXCEEDINGLY LOW

(*There is a moment of silence as they try to restrain themselves, but their glee bursts forth and they sing:*)

"I TOLD YOU SO"

GERALD. (*with HELGA responsively*)
FOUR LITTLE WORDS
I LOVE TO SAY
TO BRIGHTEN UP
MY DARKEST DAY
ARE, AT THIS POINT
QUITE APROPOS
I TOLD YOU SO

HELGA.
SHE'S BETTER OFF

GERALD.
HE'S BETTER OFF

WE'RE BETTER OFF   WE'RE BETTER OFF
SHE'S BETTER OFF

                         HE'S BETTER OFF
WE'RE BETTER OFF   WE'RE BETTER OFF
 GERALD. (*with HELGA responsively*)
THOUGH OTHERS SAY
IT GIVES THEM PAIN
TO RUB IT IN
WITH GREAT DISDAIN
I LET THEM CRINGE
THE WHILE I CROW
I TOLD YOU SO!
 GERALD.
HOW DEAR WHEN YOU PUT A LITTLE TEAR IN IT
 HELGA. (*tearfully*)
I TOLD YOU SO
 GERALD.
HOW SWEET WHEN YOU PUT A LITTLE CHEER IN IT
 HELGA. (*cheerfully*)
I TOLD YOU SO
 GERALD.
HOW NICE WITH A TEENY WEENY SNEER IN IT
 HELGA. (*sneerfully*)
I TOLD YOU SO
 GERALD.
I TOLD YOU SO
 BOTH.
I TOLD YOU SO

SHE'S BETTER OFF
HE'S BETTER OFF
WE'RE BETTER OFF

SHE'S BETTER OFF
HE'S BETTER OFF
WE'RE BETTER OFF
 GERALD. (*with HELGA, responsively*)
AS WE FORETOLD
IT'S COME TO PASS
THIS LOVE AFFAIR
IS ON ITS ASS
 HELGA.
ASS
 GERALD.
AS MORE APART THEY'VE COME TO GROW

HELGA.
THAT'S TRUE
GERALD.
LET US RECALL SOME MONTHS AGO
HELGA.
JA, DO
GERALD.
WHEN I WAS HEARD TO HOLLER, "NO!"
HELGA.
ME, TOO
GERALD.
AND NO IT IS
HELGA.
AND SO IT IS
BOTH.
I TOLD YOU SO
I TOLD YOU SO
I TOLD YOU SO!!
(*They BOTH bow.*)

[MUSIC NO. 13A — "I TOLD YOU SO" PLAYOFF]

SCENE 9

Backstage at the hotel ballroom — identical to Scene 1.
AT RISE: *Through the curtains, COUPLES can be seen dancing.*
    Now the TWO STAGEHANDS bring the larger-than-life
    photo of TESS and set it down where we saw it in Scene 1.
    Then the dancing ends and the CHAIRPERSON'S VOICE
    is heard:

CHAIRPERSON. Will the waiters please finish clearing the tables
so we can begin the award ceremony? —

(*Now, from the wings, TESS enters, wearing the same evening
    dress we saw in Scene 1. She turns to the wings behind her.*)

TESS. Hurry up, Sam — everybody will think I'm trying to
make an entrance. (*SAM enters, dressed in a smoking jacket and
carrying a program.*)
    SAM. (*He checks his watch.*) There's still plenty of time. (*dur-*

ing the following, he will take out his pen and begin sketching on the back of his program.)

TESS. No thanks to you. You took longer getting dressed than I did.

SAM. I couldn't find my tux. How was I supposed to know that Helga pressed it and put it back in your closet? Where the hell was she, anyway?

TESS. (*indicating the curtains*) In there. I got her a ticket because she feels totally responsible for my winning this award. (*noticing what he's doing*) What are you doing?

SAM. I got an idea for the strip.

TESS. Don't tell me you're bored already.

SAM. Actually, it's pretty relevant.

TESS. I'll bet.

SAM. You want to hear it?

TESS. No thank you.

SAM. Katz says: "There's an award for everything these days— movies, plays, books, *women,* dogs, floor lamps, aluminum siding—there's even a new award awarded for the best award of the year. So what else is new."

TESS. Very relevant. There's a pretty good crowd out there—

SAM. This damn tie's choking me—Helga must've shrunk it. Tess, listen—I really ought to get out of here—

TESS. You're not thinking of running that strip, are you?

SAM. Look, Tess, I couldn't be happier that they named you the Woman of the Year, but you have to admit this award business is getting slightly out of hand.

TESS. I wonder if you'd feel the same way if they came up with a Cartoonist of the Year award.

SAM. They already have. And it just so happens that I won it.

TESS. You did? Why didn't you tell me?

SAM. I did.

TESS. I didn't hear you.

SAM. You never do.

CHAIRPERSON. Please be seated, Ladies and Gentlemen, we're about to begin.

SAM. They won't ask me to say anything, will they?

TESS. (*preoccupied*) I don't see why—

SAM. I gotta get out of here—

TESS. What did you say?

SAM. I can't stay here!

TESS. What are you talking about? Of course you're staying!

SAM. No, I'm not. But I'll tell you what — meet me in two hours for dinner — just the two of us. Is it a date?

TESS. Are you crazy? You *have* to make an appearance tonight, Sam — everyone's expecting to see you. What can I tell them?

SAM. Just tell them — (*his phony Chinese again*) Cow dung chow fon cooey — !

TESS. (*angered*) Oh, Sam, for Chrissake — !

SAM. I don't give a *goddam* what you tell them! Tell them anything you goddam please! Tell them I had something important to do.

TESS. (*quickly*) Who'd believe that you had anything that was important enough to — (*She stops, realizing what she's said, he freezes, as if struck in the face.*)

CHAIRPERSON. Ladies and Gentlemen, we now come to the moment we've all been waiting for —

[MUSIC NO. 14 — FINALE ACT I]

TESS. Are you staying here with me or not, Sam?

CHAIRPERSON. — the presentation of this year's award to the Woman of the Year — (*applause*)

SAM. Wouldn't all those people out there be surprised to learn that the Woman of the Year isn't much of a woman at all? (*He turns to go.*) Goodbye, Tess. (*And he's gone. TESS is lost and confused for a moment. She takes a few steps.*)

CHAIRPERSON. — This year's winner has not only achieved a phenomenal success as a broadcast journalist, a field heretofore dominated by men, but she has also, through her blissfully happy marriage, proven beyond all doubt that today's woman can be successful both in her career and her marriage — (*TESS comes DS. and sings:*)

"WOMAN OF THE YEAR" (Reprise)

TESS.
IT'S MY NIGHT, SAMMY
ALL MINE, SAMMY
AND YOU CAN'T GIVE IT YOUR WELL-KNOWN
WHAMMY —

CHAIRPERSON. This award tonight comes as something of an anticlimax to a person who's already won a Pulitzer Prize, two Peabody awards and two Emmies —

TESS. Three Emmies —
YOU DON'T NEED TO BE HAPPY
OR SERENITY ITSELF
YOU DON'T NEED ANY PHOTOS
OF NIAGARA ON THE SHELF
YOU DON'T NEED ANY HUSBAND
GRINNING FROM EAR TO EAR
TO BE THE WOMAN OF THE YEAR

	WOMEN.
YOU DON'T NEED ANY CONSORT	
TO ASSURE YOU'RE A SMASH	OHH -----------------------------
YOU DON'T NEED ANY PUB THAT	OHH -----------------------------
FEATURES FEIFFER'S CORNED BEEF HASH	OHH -----------------------------
AND YOU DON'T NEED A HUSBAND	OHH -----------------------------
I DID NOT NEED A HUSBAND	
I WANT TO MAKE THAT VERY CLEAR	

SO, SAM CRAIG,
WHOEVER YOU ARE,
THOUGH YOU THINK I'M
   A SHAM
TAKE YOUR POW AND
   SHAZAM
AND GO SHOVE IT AND
   SCRAM
'CAUSE GODDAM IT, I AM
THE WOMAN —
   CHAIRPERSON. Ladies and Gentlemen — Miss Tess Harding!
   TESS.
— OF THE YEAR!

(*The curtain falls.*)
END OF ACT ONE

SCENE 1

[MUSIC NO. 15 — ENTR'ACTE]
The Inkpot.
AT RISE: [MUSIC NO. 15A — OPENING ACT II]
*Sitting in the booth, having a beer and sketching on his pad, is
SAM.*

SAM. Maury—! (*MAURY joins him.*)

MAURY. Yeah, Sam?

SAM. Where the hell did everybody go? I've never seen the joint so empty.

MAURY. They're in the kitchen. Herb Gardner's trying to recreate Al Capp's recipe for Mammy Yokum's Kickapoo Chicken. (*sees the sketch pad*) Okay if I look?

SAM. Help yourself.

MAURY. (*picks it up and studies it*) Everything's here except the first panel.

SAM. I haven't got that far yet. (*as MAURY looks puzzled*) I always do the strip backwards, Maury, didn't you know that?

MAURY. No.

SAM. Yeah. I start with the fourth panel and work my way back. In the first panel Katz will be in the saloon, talking to his buddies, and they ask him how his marriage is going.

MAURY. (*reading*) Okay, so Katz says, "Before the wedding everybody told me that in today's modern world it's much easier to live together than to get married. But in my case, the marriage part was a breeze — it's the living together that's so damn hard."

SAM. So what else is new?

MAURY. Not goin' so good, huh, Sam?

SAM. No, Maury, not so good. The funny part is now that I'm living alone again it's not so different from being married to Tess. But I had to move out — I couldn't take it any more. It was like being married to "60 Minutes" and "That's Incredible," all rolled into one.

MAURY. What'd you expect? She's famous. I heard that after the President's wife, she's the number two dame in the country. She must know practically everybody in the world.

SAM. You're telling me. It's been six months since I heard of anyone I haven't heard of. She hasn't got any time for us, Maury.

MAURY. Didn't it occur to you that it might be like that?

SAM. I don't know. I guess I tried not to think about it.

MAURY. Maybe it's not just your strip, Sam — maybe you do a lot of things that way.

SAM. What way?

MAURY. Backwards. (*glances off*) Tell me something, Sam — are you still on speaking terms with her?

SAM. I guess so.

MAURY. Good, 'cuz she's here. (*True enough, TESS has just entered. She hesitates, then joins Sam.*)

TESS. Hello, Mr. Craig. (*SAM regards her carefully, but says nothing.*) Remember me? The name's Tess Harding.

SAM. Hello, Miss Harding.

TESS. Can I buy you dinner tonight?

SAM. Tonight's not so good. I've got an N.C.S. meeting.

TESS. N.C.S.?

SAM. National Cartoonists Society.

TESS. Sounds important.

SAM. Oh, it is. In an unimportant sort of way.

TESS. Don't suppose you could duck it. Call in sick or something.

SAM. Afraid not.

TESS. Well. Moving right along and playing hard to get, I seem to be free tomorrow night and the night after that —

SAM. I've got a pretty heavy week, Tess —

TESS. Ah. Right. Mind if I sit down?

SAM. Of course not. Want a drink?

TESS. (*sitting*) No thanks. Well. I've had a pretty heavy week myself — especially last Friday.

SAM. Yes. I heard your acceptance speech went over very well.

TESS. I meant after that. It seems my fella walked out on me.

SAM. You'll be all right. Tess Harding knows how to take care of herself.

TESS. And how about Sam Craig? Does he know how to take care of *him*self?

SAM. Too soon to tell.

TESS. It's going to look a little funny, isn't it? Us living apart. People might not understand.

SAM. At first maybe, but later on they'll see the serious side.

TESS. Sam — why can't we sit down like grown up people and patch this thing up?

SAM. Because it might get to be a habit. And then we'll wind up with a patchwork quilt instead of a marriage.

TESS. Sam—can't we at least *talk* about it?

SAM. (*a beat*) You want to talk? All right. Let's talk.

TESS. Good. How about tonight? You can get out of your meeting—

SAM. What's wrong with right now?

TESS. Now? Well, I can't right now, Sam—I'm on a story. A big one.

SAM. Don't suppose you could duck it—call in sick or something—

TESS. You know I can't, Sam—it's an exclusive.

SAM. Oh, an exclusive. That's different.

TESS. Alexi Petrikov suddenly announced that he's going back to Russia and nobody knows why. I'm on my way over for an interview. (*beat*) What do you want me to do, Sam—give up my career?

SAM. No.

TESS. (*not hearing*) I'm sorry, I can't do that. I can't be a spectator—I have to be in the middle of things. (*beat*) I guess it wasn't much use, my coming over here.

SAM. That depends on what you were after.

TESS. I was sort of hoping you'd want to kiss me goodbye.

SAM. I was sort of hoping you'd ask me. (*He draws her to him and kisses her hard. When he draws back, he speaks matter-of-factly:*) Goodbye. (*He turns and goes.*)

[MUSIC NO. 16—"I WROTE THE BOOK"]

(*Left alone, she crosses to the booth and reads his sketch pad. MAURY joins her.*)

MAURY. Can I get you anything, Mrs. Craig?

TESS. It looks like it's "Miss Harding" again, Maury.

MAURY. No kidding. Since when?

TESS. Ten, maybe twelve seconds. (*MAURY goes and she sings:*)

"*I WROTE THE BOOK*"

TESS. (*verse*)
TO NAME ME WOMAN OF THE YEAR
WASN'T WHAT YOU'D CALL A FLUKE
THEY TELL ME THAT I WON IT IN A BREEZE
SO, THE LADIES SHOULD BE THRILLED

THEIR EXPECTATIONS ARE FULFILLED
AS I'M BROADENING MY FIELD OF EXPERTISE

(*refrain*)
I WROTE THE BOOK
ON HOW TO BE COOL
I WROTE THE BOOK
ON HOW TO BE STRONG
I WROTE THE BOOK
ON HOW TO INTERPRET THE NEWS
AND NEVER BE WRONG

I WROTE THE BOOK
ON HOW TO BE TOUGH
I WROTE THE BOOK
ON HOW TO BE TERSE
I WROTE THE BOOK
ON EVERY SUBTEXTUAL PHRASE
IN ELIOT'S VERSE

I WROTE THE BOOK
ON HOW TO HAVE CLASS
I WROTE THE BOOK
ON HOW TO HAVE CLOUT
I WROTE THE BOOK
ON READING GOVERNMENT PAMPHLETS
AND DOPING THEM OUT

SO WHEN IT COMES TO LOSING A MAN
YOU'LL FIND IT UNSURPRISINGLY TRUE
THAT LAST WEEK
I WROTE THAT BOOK, TOO

(*The FOUR CARTOONISTS—PHIL, ABBOTT, ELLIS and
    PINKY—enter from the kitchen. They stop when they see
    TESS.*)

PHIL. Tess. We thought Sam was here.
TESS. I thought he was, too. (*a pause*)
ABBOTT. You look good, Tess—
ELLIS. Yeah, you sure do—
PINKY. Yeah—(*another pause*)

TESS. So. It looks like Brenda Starr turned out to be Broom-
hilda.

PHIL. Are you kidding? You're Tess Harding. You're going to handle this the same way you do everything else. (*They sing the second chorus with TESS:*)

CARTOONISTS.

YOU WROTE THE BOOK	TESS.
ON HOW TO BE BRISK	THAT'S TRUE
YOU WROTE THE BOOK	
ON HOW TO BE BRIGHT	THAT, TOO
YOU WROTE THE BOOK	
ON SEEING NEW DELHI	
BY DAY	
AND	(*patter*)
	I-always-remember-what-
	Socrates-said,-a-brain-
	doesn't-keep-a-companion-
	in-bed.
– THE BOOK	
ON HOW TO BE CHIC	C'est vrai!
SHE WROTE THE BOOK	
ON HOW TO BE SMART	I'll say
SHE WROTE THE BOOK	
ON HOW TO EVALUATE	
TRENDS	
IN	(*patter*)
	As-Thomas-Aquinas-was-
	told-by-his-Nurse,-a-
	genius-IQ-is-a-terrible-
	curse!

TESS.

– THE BOOK	
ON HOW TO HAVE STYLE	
I WROTE THE BOOK	MEN.
ON WISDOM AND WIT	WIT!
I WROTE THE BOOK	
ON EVERY GREAT	
ENGLISH STATESMAN	
FROM CHURCHILL TO	OOH . . . OOH!
PITT	
SO WHEN IT COMES TO	DOOT DOO DOO DOOT
LOSING A MAN	DOO
YOU'LL FIND IT UNSUR-	DOOT DOO DOO DOOT
PRISINGLY TRUE	DOO
THAT LAST WEEK	

I WROTE THAT BOOK,
  TOO
(*dance*)
  MEN.
OO-OO-OO-OO —
SO WHEN IT COMES TO LOSING A MAN
YOU'LL FIND IT (HUM) UNSURPRISINGLY TRUE —
  TESS.
THAT LAST WEEK
I WROTE THAT BOOK, TOO.
  MEN.
THAT LAST WEEK
SHE WROTE THAT BOOK, TOO!!

[MUSIC NO. 16A — BALLET CLASS]

SCENE 2

A ballet rehearsal room, including mirrors and barres.
AT RISE: *ALEXI and SEVERAL DANCERS are warming up*
  as TESS enters, speaking into a microphone that is con-
  nected to a tape recorder held on her shoulder.

TESS. This is Tess Harding at the Manhattan headquarters of
Ballet America. The ballet world was stunned today by the an-
nouncement that Alexi Petrikov, who defected from his native
Russia six months ago, has decided to return there right away.
So far, Petrikov has not yet offered any explanation. (*She ap-*
proaches ALEXI.) Alexi — can you talk to me for a minute?

ALEXI. (*heavy Russian accent; while dancing*) For you, my
angel, I am refusing nothing.

TESS. I must say, Alexi, your English has greatly improved in
the last few months.

ALEXI. Yes, isn't she?

BALLET MISTRESS. (*claps twice*) Un-Du-Twa — Four!

TESS. Alexi, is it true you're returning to Russia?

ALEXI. Extremely true. I am to be giving only one performance tomorrow and then I am going back.

TESS. That must make you very unhappy.

ALEXI. *Un*happy? No, I am being the opposite! I am very
happy! I am never *being* so happy! I am going around saying
"ha-ha-ha!" all day long!

TESS. But, why on earth would you be happy going back?

ALEXI. Because I cannot live without her!

TESS. Without who?

ALEXI. Without *whom* — is being the object of the preposition —

TESS. *Whom* is it you cannot live without?

ALEXI. My wife, of course!

TESS. Your wife?

ALEXI. Whom else?

TESS. But, Alexi, what about your work? Do you mean you're willing to abandon your brilliant new career just for a marriage?

ALEXI. Tess, my angel, dancing is nice. Is beautiful. Is bringing happiness. But is only dancing. Is not to be confused with *life!* I think, perhaps, you do not understand this. Is why you are not so happy. I read the columns —

TESS. (*quickly*) Let's get back to your wife, Alexi —

ALEXI. *I* am getting back. You are staying here. Tessitchka, there is something you must learn: [MUSIC NO. 17 — "HAPPY IN THE MORNING"] After a good performance I am going to bed happy. But with my wife, I am waking *up* happy! Believe me, my angel, is much *more* important! (*He sings:*)

"HAPPY IN THE MORNING"

ALEXI.
HAPPY IN THE MORNING
WHAT A THRILL, O —
'BLIGING THE BELOVED
ON YOUR PILLOW
YOU CAN SUFFER THROUGH
THE EVENING, THEN —
TOMORROW YOU'LL BE
BEGINNING OVER AGAIN

BALLET MISTRESS. Places!

ALEXI.
HAPPY IN THE MORNING
LAUGHING, JOKING
HAPPY IN THE MORNING
KISSING, STROKING
READY TO ENDURE WHATEVER LIES AHEAD
JUMPING OUT OF BED

SO HAPPY IN THE EARLY
MORNING HOUR

SOAPING WITH A LOVED ONE
IN THE SHOWER
FEELING IN YOUR CAREFREE HEART
YOU'RE GETTING OFF
TO A VERY GOOD START
(*a glare from the BALLET MISTRESS*)

TESS. I'm going, I'm going!

ALEXI.
AND THEN
SO WHAT IF YOU'RE ASSAULTED BY SOME PRUNE
WHICH MAKES YOU HAVE A LOUSY AFTERNOON?
SO WHAT IF SOME MISFORTUNE EVENING BRINGS?
YOU CAN WORK OUT
ON YOUR INNER SPRINGS
KNOWING AS YOU FALL ASLEEP
THAT WHEN THE ROBIN SINGS
YOU WILL BE—

—HAPPY IN THE MORNING
WITH YOUR LOVER
TICK-A-LING YOUR TOES
BENEATH THE COVER
MISERY MAY COME, BUT THEN
YOU KNOW TOMORROW YOU'LL BE HAPPY
HAPPY IN THE MORNING
HAPPILY BEGINNING OVER AGAIN!

TESS. Now let me get this straight, Alexi—are you saying you're willing to abandon everything you slaved and sacrificed for, are you saying you'd give all that up just so you could feel happy in the morning?

ALEXI. Absolutely!

TESS. (*regards him with total bewilderment*) Alexi—one of us is a total idiot.

ALEXI. Absolutely! (*BALLET MISTRESS comes to them.*)

TESS. I'm going, I'm going!

BALLET MISTRESS. Continue!! (*ALEXI and the OTHER DANCERS now do the final chorus:*)

ALEXI.
HAPPY IN THE MORNING
WHAT A THRILL, O—
'BLIGING THE BELOVED ON YOUR PILLOW
SORRORS MAY BEFALL, BUT THEN
YOU KNOW TOMORROW YOU'LL BE HAPPY

BALLERINA.
HAPPY IN THE MORNING
ALEXI.
HAPPILY BEGINNING OVER AGAIN
(*dance*)
    ALL. Happy!!!! (*After song:*)
    BALLET MISTRESS. One more time!

[MUSIC NO. 18—"SOMETIMES A DAY GOES BY" INTRO]

(*The lights fade.*)

SCENE 3

SAM's studio.
AT RISE: *SAM is at his work table, sketching. He is alone except
    for the large stuffed facsimile of KATZ.*

    SAM. C'mon, Katz—be a little patient, will you? I've done
everything except the first panel. You wouldn't think I'd still
have so much trouble drawing hands after all these years, would
you? Okay, want to hear it? (*He's finished sketching and now
reads from the page.*) You go to a lawyer because you want a
divorce—(*looks at KATZ*) That's what I said—A divorce.
(*reads*) On what grounds, the lawyer wants to know, but you
can't think of any. "In that case," says the lawyer, "you'd better
get the latest thing—a no-fault divorce." "What's a no-fault
divorce?" you want to know, and the lawyer says: "Leaving the
scene of an accident." So what else is new? (*looks up*) Funny?—
Pretty funny—(*a beat*) Not so funny. What the hell do you
know, Katz? How would *you* like to be married to someone
who's more *successful,* more *important,* makes more *money*
than you—someone who's never around when you need her
because she's too busy travelling all over the goddam world, and
who spends more time with Yuri Andropov, than she does with
you?! Remember how good it was, Katz? Before she came
along? No arguments, no fights, no yelling and screaming—
remember how goddam *boring* it was?!

[MUSIC NO. 18—"SOMETIMES A DAY GOES BY"]

(*He becomes contemplative and he sings:*)

"SOMETIMES A DAY GOES BY"

SAM.
SOMETIMES A DAY GOES BY
ONE WHOLE ENTIRE DAY
WHEN I DON'T THINK OF HER

TWENTY-FOUR HOURS PASS
I LOOK AROUND AND FIND
THAT I HAVEN'T THOUGHT OF HER

NOT EVEN WHEN
I'M SOMEWHERE WE USED TO GO
NOT EVEN IF
THAT'S SOMEONE WE USED TO KNOW

IT'S HARDLY EVERY DAY
IT'S MOST UNUSUAL
IN FACT, I CAN'T REMEMBER WHEN

BUT, SOMETIMES A DAY GOES BY
WHEN I DON'T THINK OF HER

'TIL MORNING COMES AND THEN—
THERE SHE IS AGAIN
(*music under*)
(*spoken*) I'm going out for some air. You get the lights, Katz.
(*As he walks* DS., *the street drop comes in behind him. He sings:*)
NOT EVEN WHEN
I'M SOMEWHERE WE USED TO GO
NOT EVEN IF
THAT'S SOMEONE WE USED TO KNOW

IT'S HARDLY EVERY DAY
IT'S MOST UNUSUAL
IN FACT, I CAN'T REMEMBER WHEN

BUT, SOMETIMES A DAY GOES BY
WHEN I DON'T THINK OF HER

'TIL MORNING COMES AND THEN—
THERE SHE IS AGAIN

(*The lights fade.*)

[MUSIC NO. 18A — "SOMETIMES A DAY GOES BY" UTILITY]

SCENE 4

*The living room-kitchen of LARRY's house, somewhere in
Colorado. It's a fine, rustic room, at the center of which
is a large, wood-burning stove.*

AT RISE: *JAN, dressed in an old, formless robe, her hair up in
rollers, sits on a stool facing front. A moment later her
husband, LARRY, wearing a tweed jacket with leather
elbow patches, enters, carrying a load of wood for the stove.*

JAN. It's almost noon, Larry. For someone who's supposed to
get up at three-thirty every day she's certainly sleeping late.

LARRY. She didn't arrive until two in the morning. (*observing
her*) She could come down any minute, Jan — don't you think
you ought to get ready?

JAN. (*a beat*) I'm ready.

LARRY. What about the house?

JAN. (*looks around*) It's ready, too.

LARRY. Come on, Jan. You're always so neat and tidy, everything is so clean you could eat off it. But ever since yesterday,
when she called to say she was coming out, you've been acting
very oddly. Just because she happens to be my ex-wife —

JAN. (*to an imaginary third party*) Ex-wife, he says. (*to
LARRY*) Larry, I can deal with an ex-wife. But that happens to
be Tess Harding up there. She's known five Presidents, Larry —
one of them extremely well, I understand —

LARRY. Jan —

JAN. — She's made the best-dressed list nine years straight —
she's been on more magazine covers than Miss Piggy — they're
actually naming a perfume after her —

LARRY. Jan —

JAN. — At my best, Larry, at my *very best* — to her I'd look
like this anyway, so what's the use?

LARRY. Jan —

JAN. What's she doing here, Larry? Tell me that.

LARRY. She didn't say.

JAN. (*to the third person*) She didn't say.

LARRY. I hate it when you do that —

JAN. Do what?

LARRY. Talk to someone who isn't here.

JAN. (*to the third person*) He hates it. (*to LARRY*) She must've said *some*thing, Larry—

LARRY. (*He goes to throw another log into the stove.*) If you wanted to know so badly you should've waited up last night.

JAN. I can't stay awake that late. All I can say is it's pretty strange.

LARRY. What is?

JAN. She invites herself all the way out to Colorado, arrives at two in the morning and goes straight to bed without any explanation.

LARRY. First of all, she did not invite herself. We *asked* her to come out and stay with us.

JAN. Sure, eleven years ago! (*She stares at him for a moment.*) There's something I've been meaning to ask you, Larry: You were married to her, and then you married me. I mean, you left Tess Harding, the Woman of the Year, and you married me. Larry—(*a beat*) Who *are* you?

LARRY. (*looking up*) She's up—I can hear her moving around—

JAN. Oh my God. I'm so nervous I'm getting split ends.

LARRY. (*He goes to feed the stove again.*) Will you please relax? Everything'll be all right if you just relax. Look at me— I'm relaxed, aren't I?

JAN. Is that why you just threw your galoshes into the stove?

LARRY. (*He races back to the stove, raises the lid, but it's too late.*) Damn. (*And now TESS appears, in pants, her hair tied back, looking wonderful.*)

TESS. Good morning! Good morning! Boy, did I sleep! It's got to be the air! Larry! Oh, Larry, I'm so glad to see you—(*She puts her arms around him and gives him a big kiss. During which LARRY shrugs at JAN as she glares back. Finally TESS turns to JAN.*) And you must be Jane.

JAN. Jan.

TESS. Jan. Of course you are. Him Larry, you Jan. (*a forced laugh which dies painfully*) What a charming room! The entire house is so—warm and—and *lived* in. It's exactly the way I pictured it—with something wonderful cooking on the stove— what's that delightful smell?

JAN. Larry's galoshes.

LARRY. You must be hungry, Tess—what would you like for lunch?

TESS. Breakfast.

JAN. How about a croissant?

TESS. Croissant? I don't believe it!

LARRY. This is Colorado, Tess, not Outer Mongolia. Jan makes them herself.

TESS. You're kidding! Can I watch?

JAN. I'm afraid they're already made. I run up a batch every couple of months and then I freeze them.

TESS. My God, that's incredible. I couldn't do that if my life depended on it. I wouldn't even know how to start.

LARRY. What, how to make a croissant?

TESS. No, how to freeze them. (*As JAN moves over to the kitchen to prepare breakfast, TESS studies LARRY.*) You look pretty good, Larry. Pretty damn good. Frankly, I wasn't sure what to expect. Sixteen years is a long time.

LARRY. You look pretty damn good yourself. You're thinner than you look on TV.

TESS. The tube does that to you. And don't you have a daughter? What's her name—Joan?

JAN. June.

TESS. Right. She's how old now—ten, eleven?

LARRY. Fifteen, if you can believe that. She's in Vail, skiing. And how's Sam?

TESS. (*She turns and looks him straight in the eye.*) He left me. (*There's an awkward silence as LARRY and JAN look at her, at each other, then back at her again. Finally:*)

JAN. Larry—why don't you go out and get some more wood for the stove.

LARRY. The wood-box is full now, babe.

JAN. Then why don't you just go out?

LARRY. Oh. Yeah. (*He starts out.*) I'll get some more wood for the stove. (*And he's gone. TESS has seated herself on one of the stools and now regards her hands, dejectedly.*)

JAN. You okay?

TESS. Not particularly.

JAN. How about a cup of coffee?

TESS. No—

JAN. I've got some Polish vodka in the freezer—

TESS. Now you're talking. (*JAN goes to the freezer, pulls out a bottle, then gets two glasses, hurries back on the run.*)

JAN. Okay, what happened? (*She pours a healthy shot for each.*)

TESS. I don't know. One minute we were deliriously happy,

and the next we were fighting about everything. At first I thought he was the one who was wrong. But last week someone I know gave up everything I thought was important just to save his marriage. Jan! *I* must be the one who's wrong!

JAN. That's ridiculous. How do you know?

TESS. Little things.

JAN. Such as what?

TESS. My husband walked out on me.

JAN. (*considering*) Yeah—that's one way of telling.

TESS. And then it occurred to me that the most happily married man I knew was my ex-husband. Show me what to do, Jan—you know how to make a man happy—tell it to me once, I'm a quick study.

JAN. What can I tell you? You're Tess Harding, for God's sake—you know everything!

TESS. Yeah, but that's *all* I know. I can't *do* anything. Look at you—you can *do* everything.

[MUSIC NO. 19—"THE GRASS IS ALWAYS GREENER"]

JAN. Oh, sure. Everything trivial. I've never done anything really important with my life, the way you have. (*She sings:*)

"THE GRASS IS ALWAYS GREENER"

JAN.
I BET YOUR FRIENDS ARE ALL CELEBRITIES
THAT'S WONDERFUL!
TESS.
WHAT'S SO WONDERFUL?
YOU CAN MAKE A POT ROAST
THAT'S WONDERFUL!
JAN.
WHAT'S SO WONDERFUL
FIRST, YOU BROWN AN ONION

IS YOUR PICTURE UP AT SARDI'S?
THAT'S WONDERFUL!
TESS.
WHAT'S SO WONDERFUL
YOU CAN CLEAN AN OVEN
THAT'S WONDERFUL!

JAN.
WHAT'S SO WONDERFUL!
FIRST, YOU GET THE E.Z. OFF
　BOTH.
AH, THE GRASS IS ALWAYS GREENER
ON SOMEBODY ELSE'S ESTATE!
AH, THE MEAT IS ALWAYS LEANER
ON SOMEBODY ELSE'S DINNER PLATE!
　TESS.
BUT, YOU CAN SEW A BUTTON ON
THAT'S WONDERFUL!
　JAN.
WHAT'S SO WONDERFUL?
BET YOU'VE BEEN TO DISCOS
THAT'S WONDERFUL!
　TESS.
WHAT'S SO WONDERFUL?
FIRST YOU TAKE A VALIUM

I CAN SEE YOU PLANNING PICNICS
THAT'S WONDERFUL!
　JAN.
WHAT'S SO WONDERFUL?
EATING AT THE WHITE HOUSE
THAT'S WONDERFUL!
　TESS.
WHAT'S SO WONDERFUL?
FIRST THEY PASS THE JELLY BEANS
　BOTH.
AH, THE GRASS IS ALWAYS GREENER
ON SOMEBODY ELSE'S FRONT LAWN
AH, SOMEBODY ELSE'S WEINER
ALWAYS HAS A LOT MORE RELISH ON!
　JAN.
YOU SAVED THE WHALES IN NEWFOUNDLAND
THAT'S WONDERFUL!
　TESS.
WHAT'S SO WONDERFUL?
YOU CAN RUN A HOUSEHOLD
THAT'S WONDERFUL!
　JAN.
WHAT'S SO WONDERFUL?
FIRST, YOU HAVE A BREAKDOWN

YOU'RE ALWAYS IN THE MAGAZINES
THAT'S WONDERFUL!
    Tess.
WHAT'S SO WONDERFUL?
YOU CAN HOLD A HUSBAND
THAT'S WONDERFUL!
    Jan.
WHAT'S SO WONDERFUL?
THERE'S MORE TO LIFE THAN HUSBANDS
    Tess.
I COULD USE A HUSBAND
    Jan.
YOU CAN HAVE MY HUSBAND
    Tess.
(*mumbling*)
I'VE ALREADY HAD YOUR HUSBAND—
    Both.
AH, IT MAKES YOU KIND OF TEARY
AH, THINK ABOUT IT DEARIE
THE GRASS IS ALWAYS GREENER
IN SOMEONE ELSE'S YARD!

IT'S HARD!

[MUSIC NO. 20—"THE GRASS IS ALWAYS GREENER" ENCORE]

(*encore*)

    Jan.
I BET YOU ALWAYS RIDE IN LIMOUSINES
THAT'S WONDERFUL!
    Tess.
WHAT'S SO WONDERFUL?
YOU'VE GOT TIME FOR LUNCHEONS
THAT'S WONDERFUL!
    Jan.
WHAT'S SO WONDERFUL?
FIRST, YOU SELL THE TUPPERWARE

THE PUBLIC WANTS YOUR AUTOGRAPH
THAT'S WONDERFUL!
    Tess.
WHAT'S SO WONDERFUL?

YOU RAISED A TEEN-AGE DAUGHTER
THAT'S WONDERFUL!
 JAN.
WHAT'S SO WONDERFUL?
FIRST, YOU FIND HER DIAPHRAGM
 BOTH.
AH, THE GRASS IS ALWAYS GREENER
WHERE SOME OTHER TENANT PAYS RENT!
AH, THE TEETH ARE ALWAYS CLEANER
IN SOMEBODY ELSE'S POLIDENT!
 TESS.
DO YOU KNOW WHO YOUR NEIGHBORS ARE?
THAT'S WONDERFUL!
 JAN.
WHAT'S SO WONDERFUL?
YOU KNOW RONA BARRETT
THAT'S WONDERFUL!
 TESS.
WHAT'S SO WONDERFUL?
FIRST, YOU KEEP YOUR MOUTH SHUT

I BET YOU SQUEEZE THE CHARMIN
THAT'S WONDERFUL!
 JAN.
WHAT'S SO WONDERFUL?
YOU CAN MAKE A HEADLINE
THAT'S WONDERFUL!
 TESS.
WHAT'S SO WONDERFUL?
I'D RATHER MAKE A POT ROAST
 JAN.
SO, GO AND BROWN AN ONION
 TESS.
AND HAVE SOME PEACE AND QUIET
 JAN.
YOU'VE ALREADY HAD MY HUSBAND
 BOTH.
AH, EVERYONE'S A VICTIM
OF THIS DUCKY LITTLE DICTUM
THE GRASS IS ALWAYS GREENER
IN SOMEONE ELSE'S YARD!

IT'S HARD!!

(*After song: LARRY re-enters.*)

TESS. Larry! You don't know how lucky you are! Oh, Jan, you've given me a wonderful idea! And, both of you, make sure you watch my show tomorrow morning! (*She goes.*)

LARRY. She's really something, isn't she, Jane?

JAN. Jan.

[MUSIC NO. 20B — AFTER COLORADO]

(*Lights out. In the darkness, the following announcement is heard:*)

TV ANNOUNCER. — Coming up after a word from your local stations — the "Early Bird" show from New York, with anchorpersons Tess Harding and Chip Salisbury — (*Lights back up on:*)

SCENE 5

The TV Studio, with the anchor desk, as before, and beside it, a kitchen unit, complete with counter, sink, stove, and, over these, a large wall oven.

AT RISE: *There is all of the activity that usually precedes a network broadcast — a CREW including CAMERAMEN, SOUNDMEN, FLOOR MANAGERS, GRIPS and OTHERS are putting last-minute touches on the set. GERALD enters with a clipboard and stops, center, occupying himself with checking off various items on a list. After a moment, CHIP enters, looking frazzled.*

CHIP. Gerald! Will you please tell me what the heck's going on? She calls me from Colorado and says to dig out the kitchen set. The *kitchen* set, for gosh sakes! Doesn't she know that kitchen sets are *death?* You don't see Jane Pauley using a kitchen set! You don't see Diane Sawyer using a kitchen set! Sure, Phil Donahue used one once, but he was proving that breakfast causes cancer. What's she trying to do, shoot down our ratings?

GERALD. I don't think she cares about our ratings anymore.

CHIP. What are you talking about?

GERALD. She called me from Colorado, too — she asked me to

make sure that Mr. Craig watches the show today, she said she has a surprise for him.

CHIP. What kind of a surprise? I *hate* surprises!

(*Now HELGA enters, carrying an apron over her arm.*)

HELGA. Gerald — Gerald, was gibt's? I am going cuckoo!

GERALD. Helga! What are you doing here?

HELGA. Miss Harding called — all the way from Avocado.

CHIP. Colorado.

HELGA. Cado, rado, what's the difference? Do you know what she told me? To bring an apron! Gerald, what does she want with an apron?

GERALD. I don't know. I don't know anything anymore. She used to tell me everything and now I'm the last to find out! It's not fair, you know, it's just not fair!

CHIP. All I can say is, she must have something pretty big planned, a real biggie. But what's she going to do in the kitchen?

GERALD. Just pray she doesn't cook anything.

(*TESS arrives on the set, dressed and made-up. She appears quite happy and oblivious of their concern.*)

TESS. Ah, Helga, there you are. And you brought the apron, that's fantastic.

HELGA. You must be careful, it is my best apron.

TESS. (*as HELGA ties the apron on her*) I'll guard it with my life, Helga, I swear. Now, I want you to stay close to me during the show —

HELGA. Really? I would rather watch channel seven — that David Hartman is such a cupcake.

TESS. Yeah, well, you'll have to miss him this once. I'm going to need your help.

GERALD. Why? What are you going to do?

TESS. You'll find out.

DIRECTOR'S VOICE. (*off*) Chip — thirty seconds to air —

CHIP. Coming! Golly, Tess, you know they don't like it when we make things up —

TESS. Just handle the opening and then introduce Tess' Corner. I'll take it from there.

DIRECTOR'S VOICE. (*off*) Ten seconds —

CHIP. I need a spritz! (*to the HAIRDRESSER who arrives*) I

smell trouble. The last time I smelled trouble, Norman Mailer used the F word seven times! — (*lights up as the show begins*) Good morning, and welcome to "Early Bird." I'm Chip Salisbury. It's seven o'clock here in New York, and we'll start the show today with our regular visit to Tess' Corner, where our resident Woman of the Year has a surprise for us. Tess? — (*Lights go out on CHIP and up on TESS in the kitchen.*)

TESS. Good morning. Today is my husband's birthday. And as a present to him I wish to make the following announcement: This is the final appearance of Tess' Corner, because it's the final appearance of Tess. From now on you'll be able to find me right here, in the kitchen. My own kitchen. And sitting across from me — just about there — will be my husband, Sam Craig. The problem is, you see, I've been having breakfast every morning with eighteen million people. And while that's earned me a 36 share in the ratings, I wound up with a zero share at home. So on this special day, I'm going to do what any relatively intelligent person should be able to do: bake a cake. —

HELGA. Oh mein Gott!

[MUSIC NO. 21 — "OPEN THE WINDOW"]

TESS. From now on, Tess' Corner will be a very private plate, shared only with you. Open the window, Sam — (*She sings:*)

"OPEN THE WINDOW, SAM"

TESS.
— OPEN THE DOOR
EARLY BIRD'S COMING HOME

I'M NOT THE VULTURE
THAT I WAS BEFORE
EARLY BIRD'S COMING HOME

RISE FROM YOUR CHAIR WITH A WELCOMING SMILE
FOR EACH LITTLE INCH, SAM
I'LL GIVE YOU A MILE

OPEN THE WINDOW, SAM
OPEN THE DOOR
EARLY BIRD'S COMING HOME!

(*music under*)

Okay now — What's Craig Claiborne got to say on the subject? — "Birthday Cake: Two cups flour, two teaspoons baking powder, two eggs separated, one teaspoon salt, one cup milk, one teaspoon vanilla, one cup sugar, one half cup shortening." What's so tough about that? (*She looks around.*) Short'nin' — short'nin' — (*As she gathers the ingredients she sings:*)

MAMMA'S LITTLE BABY LOVES BIRTHDAY, BIRTHDAY
MAMMA'S LITTLE BABY LOVES BIRTHDAY CAKE
MAMMA'S LITTLE BABY LOVES FLOUR AND
    SHORT'NIN'
MAMMA'S LITTLE BABY LOVES EGGS THAT BREAK

PUT IN THE SUGAR, PUT IN THE MILK
WHIP UP A BATTER THAT'S SMOOTH AS SILK

(*Music under; she looks back into the book.*)

Now what? — "Preheat oven to three-seventy-five." Good thinking, Craig-baby! (*She turns to the stove and stares at the numerous dials and switches.*) My God, you need a degree from M.I.T. (*She laughs, then tries a dial and the time buzzer goes off. She jumps, startled, then frantically turns all the knobs and switches, trying to turn it off. HELGA has crept onto the set, trying to stay low, out of camera range, and now reaches up and turns off the buzzer.*) How do you like that? It even has a burglar alarm. Now, then — pre-heat — (*Again, HELGA's hand reaches up and turns a knob. TESS slaps her hand.*) I'd've found it! (*turns to camera, smiling*) I found it. Okay, now to mix the batter — Let's see — (*She tears the page out of the cookbook and takes it to the counter, then picks up a teaspoon and dips it into a large canister marked "FLOUR".*) — Flour, two teaspoons — (*She spoons it into a large mixing bowl, then finds a small tin of baking powder.*) — and baking powder, two cups —

HELGA. No! —

TESS. Quiet, I can do it! (*She pours the contents into a mixing cup.*) I hope there's enough —

HELGA. Miss Harding — !

TESS. No fair helping, Helga — I want to do this all by myself. (*As she continues singing, she will add other ingredients to the mix: sugar and milk:*)

OPEN THE WINDOW, SAM
OPEN THE DOOR
EARLY BIRD'S COMING HOME

I WAS A TURKEY
NOW LOOK AT ME SOAR
EARLY BIRD'S COMING HOME

STAND BY THE STOVE
WITH A WELCOMING LOOK
AND I'LL GIVE A NEW MEANING
TO OUR BREAKFAST NOOK

(*She winks.*)

OPEN THE WINDOW, SAM
OPEN THE DOOR
EARLY BIRD'S COMING HOME

(*Music under as she continues adding to the mix.*)

(*spoken*) Okay, what's next—Shortening, one-half cup—(*sings:*)
MAMMA'S LITTLE BABY LOVES BIRTHDAY, BIRTHDAY
MAMMA'S LITTLE BABY LOVES BIRTHDAY CAKE

PUT IN VANILLA, PUT IN THE SALT,
IF THIS DOESN'T WORK IT'S CLAIBORNE'S FAULT

(*Music under as she adds these ingredients, too.*)

(*spoken*) And now, last but not least, two eggs—(*picks up two eggs*)— separated. (*With one in each hand, she places them as far apart as her arms will stretch.*) Ha, ha, just kidding, folks—(*She picks up the eggs and studies them.*) Two eggs, separated. But not divorced. (*to the eggs*) You two kids are going to get back together yet! (*looks around*) Now what?— (*As she looks, HELGA's hand shoves a hand strainer up at her; TESS takes it.*) Right, right. (*She breaks the eggs into it, holding it over the sink so the whites can seep through, leaving the yolks in the strainer.*) Yechhh! That's disgusting. (*She dumps the yolks into the bowl.*) I can't believe Julia Child started this way. Okay, now mix it all up—(*She picks up an electric handmixer and, turning it on, dips it into the bowl for a moment, then turns it off.*) Yummy. Now pour it out—(*She pours the batter into a cake pan.*) Voila, sa they say. (*She opens the oven door, puts the cake pan inside and closes the door.*) You see that, Sam? A piece of cake.

ALL.
OPEN THE WINDOW, SAM
OPEN THE DOOR
EARLY BIRD'S COMING HOME

I'M NOT THE VULTURE
THAT I WAS BEFORE
EARLY BIRD'S COMING HOME

TESS.
I'VE PUT A NEW SHINE
ON MY GOLD WEDDING BAND
SO, PUT DOWN THE FINGER
AND GIMME A HAND

ALL.
PLEASE!
OPEN THE WINDOW, SAM
OPEN THE DOOR

TESS.
EARLY BIRD'S SINGING
OF JOY SHE'LL BE BRINGING

ALL.
AS EARLY BIRD IS WINGING HER WAY BACK HOME!
HOME!
HOME!

SAM. (*entering,* L.) Get out of my way! Would you mind telling me what in the hell this is all about?

TESS. Sam! What are you doing here? I thought you'd be home watching.

SAM. I wouldn't stand too close, if I were you — (*He pulls her away from the oven.*)

CHIP. Jeeesus Christ! We're still on the air!

TESS. You wanted a wife? Now you've got one.

SAM. No kidding. You mean love, honor, cherish and obey, 'til an assignment in Istanbul do us part?

CHIP. (*to the camera*) I promised you a surprise, didn't I? Wow!!

TESS. Sam, I quit my job!

SAM. Terrific. You mean you're going to cook and clean and sew buttons on my pajamas and mop the floor and wash the windows? We won't need Helga anymore. (*to HELGA on the floor*) Maybe you can get your old job back with the Luftwaffe. (*The cake starts to ooze out of the oven.*)

TESS. *Sam, do something!!*

HAIRDRESSER. (*running to smoking stove, "spritzing"*) Clear the set! Run! Run! Clear the set! (*SAM turns off stove. The cake recedes with a groan.*)

SAM. Tess—I don't want you to quit your job, you're too damn good at it. You don't want to quit, either. You're a big phony.

TESS. (*pushing SAM aside*) Don't big phony me! I meant every word I said!

SAM. (*following TESS*) Oh, did you? Then why didn't you just tell it to me—why'd you have to say it on television? (*grabs mike boom, start imitating her*) Hi there! This is Tess Harding for "Early Bird"—telling all you wonderful folks out there in televisionland—my very most private personal business—

TESS. Stop it, Sam!

SAM. —And giving all you early worms the bird. (*raspberry*)

TESS. I said, *stop it!*

CHIP. (*to the camera*) We'll be right back with the multi-talented Piz Zadora—(*TESS picks up two eggs, misses SAM and cracks the eggs over CHIP's head. There's a moment of shocked silence. Finally:*)

TESS. You need a spritz! (*All tip-toe offstage except SAM and TESS.*)

[MUSIC NO. 22—FINALE ACT II]

SAM. Don't you see, Tess? Just because I couldn't take being married to Tess Harding, that doesn't mean I wanted you to be Mrs. Sam Craig.

TESS. What *do* you want?

SAM. You could try being Tess Harding Craig. I don't want you to stop being you. All I ever wanted was for you to leave some room in your life for me.

TESS. I love you—

SAM. So what do you say, Tess Harding Craig—do we give it a shot?—(*They sing:*)

"TABLE TALK" (Reprise)

TESS.
HOW MANY FINGERS UP?
(*holds two up*)
SAM.
TWO
TESS.
NOW LET'S CHECK YOUR HEARING.
SAM.
WHAT'S WRONG WITH MY HEARING?
TESS.
I SAID "I LOVE YOU"
SAM.
I HEAR YOU, I HEAR YOU!
(*They kiss.*)

"WOMAN OF THE YEAR" (Reprise)

SAM.
CAUSE, YOU DO HAVE A HUSBAND
TESS.
YES, I DO HAVE A HUSBAND
SAM.
SO LET'S MAKE ONE THING VERY CLEAR
TESS.
WE'LL BE—
TESS & COMPANY.
—THE COUPLE OF THE YEAR!

(*Music swells—theme from "TABLE TALK"—they begin to dance with each other. On music cue, the screen comes in— and the cartoon of KATZ and TESSIE are dancing in the same manner—and in the background, a huge, colorful sunset, into which KATZ and TESSIE eventually walk. A legend appears: "AND THEY LIVED SCRAPPILY EVER AFTER." And then: "SO WHAT ELSE IS NEW?"*)

FINAL CURTAIN

PROPS

ACT ONE

Scene 1 — Banquet

On Stage
Large banquet table
2 Tables w/candleabra lamps
6 Chairs

Scene 2 — TV Studio into Sam's Studio

On Stage
TV news desk w/2 swivel chairs

Off Left
Clipboards, yellow pads, pencils, headset, 2 sets cuecards, early-
   bird script

Off Right
6 foot ladder, make-up tray w/mirror, briefcase (Gerald) w/TV
   commentary, briefcase (Tess), hairbrush, hair spray bottle

On Stage
Sam's studio: drawing table w/3 beer cans, ashtray, cigarettes,
   playing cards, paper money
2 chairs, large can, waste basket, tall stool around drawing table
"Katz" character holding cards on stool
Small spool table D.C.
Wicker bench with small pillows L.
US. bookcase shelves: cans of pens, pencils, crayons, cartoonists
   "encyclopedia"
Large sketch pad w/"katz" drawing
US. cork board w/cartoon drawings
Small table w/pens, pencils R.

Off Left
Portable TV, can of beer

Scene 3 — Tess' Office

On Stage
Tess' desk w/phone, 2 letters C.
Swivel chair, office chair

Gerald desk w/phone, letters, pad, pencils L.
Office chair
File cabinet, large painting U.C.

Off Left
Newspaper, briefcase (Gerald)
Briefcase, purse (Tess) w/beeper, compact, datebook, pen

Scene 4 — Sam's Studio

On Stage
Telephone, small artist's sketch pad on drawing table

Off Right
Briefcase (Gerald) w/folder typed letters, pen

Scene 5 — Inkpot Bar

On Stage
Bar banquette booth w/beer bottles, ashtray, cards R.
Bar stool
Pool table w/5 cue sticks, balls U.C.
Bar w/liquor & beer bottles, various glasses, trays L.
Champagne bottle & glass, filled beer bottle & stein, slop bucket
     & towel
Small tray w/bourbon bottle (nearly empty) & 2 glasses
Magic cards, bar rag, cigarettes, ashtray
"Dolly" slider on bar

Off Left
2 swivel bar stools
Purse (Tess) w/beeper, coins, compact, comb, keys

Scene 6 — Tess' Apartment

On Stage
Bed w/pillows, blanket R.
Small shelf w/telephone, vase of flowers
Desk w/phone (long receiver cord), message pad, pencils, 2 let-
     ters C.
Swivel desk chair
Sofa & small table L.
Fireplace, Tess painting U.C.

Off Left
Duffel bag, champagne bucket w/bottle, 2 glasses; bed pillow, briefcase (Gerald) w/newswire tear-sheets, Spanish script
Large basket of flowers w/card, large tray w/12 champagne glasses, 2 champagne bottles & glass, 3 plates w/food, autograph book & pen

Scene 7—"It Isn't Working"

On Stage
Bar banquette w/phone, ashtray, cards R.
TV news desk w/swivel chair, pad & pencil L.

Off Right
Clipboard, script, phone, 5 brown store bags w/phone receivers, 1 brown bag

Off Left
Hair spray bottle

Scene 8—Tess' Apartment

On Stage
On bed: news magazine, reference books, clipboard, pencil
On desk: 2 typed letters, pen, pad
On fireplace: bourbon bottle & glass

Off Left
Duffel bag, raincoat, tray w/2 teacups, teapot
Door slam

Scene 9—Banquet

Off Right
Table, 2 chairs

Off Left
Program & pen, small pad

ACT TWO

Scene 1—Inkpot

On Stage
On banquette: tray w/2 glasses, bar-rag

On bar: bourbon bottle, glass, ashtray, cigarettes, matches,
 small sketch pad
Bar stool
Various bottles, trays

Scene 2 — Ballet Studio

Off Right
6 Chairs

Off Left
Ballet Mistress baton-stick
Tape recorder case w/mic

Scene 3 — Sam's Studio

On Stage
Medium sketch pad on drawing table, pencils

Scene 4 — Colorado

On Stage
Kitchen counter w/coffee pot & mug D.R.
Tall stool
Refrigerator w/orange juice, vodka bottle, croissants in pan
 U.R.
Wood-burning country stove w/moveable lid U.C.
Coffee mug
Wood-box
Counter w/sink, 2 glasses, towels D.L.
Tall stool
Two racks of pot, pans attached to L. counter

Off Right
2 small loads of wood logs
Galoshes

Scene 5 — TV Studio

On Stage
Colorado kitchen converts to modern kitchen set

Off Left
2 large trays, 8 large stirring spoons, cue cards, apron, cake
 (stuffed cloth)

Recipe book

Off Right
Script, briefcase (Gerald), boom mike (practical), make-up tray
    hair spray bottle
Large tray w/pitcher of milk, bowl of eggs, crisco, salt, vanill
Large tray w/flour, sugar, baking powder
Metal baking pan w/3 measuring cups, 1 set of measuring spoon
Large mixing bowl w/strainer, teaspoon, measuring cup, electri
    hand mixer
Two plastic buckets with damp towels